ANGEL CREEK PRESS

Christmas in Clear Creek by Kit Morgan

Cover Design and Interior Format

Christmas
IN
Clear Creek

KIT MORGAN

Other Titles in this Series

For a complete list of Kit's books check out her website at **www.authorkitmorgan.com**

Welcome to Clear Creek!

If this is your first Kit Morgan book about the town of Clear Creek, then you're in for a treat! This story can stand alone – you can get to know this quirky little town through the eyes of Bowen Drake and Elsie Waller, and meet the townsfolk right along with them! If you've followed the Prairie Bride Series this far, then you'll be laughing as usual at the antics of the Cooke brothers and the rest of Clear Creek's unusual residents!

Those of you with an adventurous spirit can backtrack and begin the adventure with His Prairie Princess, the first book in the Prairie Bride Series, and go from there! Christmas in Clear Creek wraps up the series and opens the door for the next series, Prairie Grooms!

One

Clear Creek, Oregon Territory, November 28th, 1858

BOWEN DRAKE HAD A GIFT. Unfortunately, he didn't want it.

Not that it was a bad gift, mind you – most would say it was in fact a very good gift, even a great one. But it hadn't served Bowen in the manner in which he'd hoped, and had left him wandering for years as a lost soul, looking for someplace to belong. Though it didn't help that he'd been looking in all the wrong places – on purpose.

What drives a man to *want* to be bad?

Well, Bowen had his reasons. He and his father didn't get along well anymore, owing to Bowen blaming him for his mother's death. After all, if Franklin Drake M.D., a prominent Philadelphia physician, hadn't been out treating and saving everyone and their grandmother from influenza in the winter of '48, then perhaps he'd have had time to save his own wife (and *Bowen's* mother) from the disease. But no, Doc Drake was never home to help her – too busy being a hero to the city.

To compound the problem, Mrs. Drake's death was as hard on the doctor as it was on Bowen. Dr. Drake took to drinking to cope with the loss – and perhaps his own guilt – which led Bowen to take to leaving. Bowen was greatly gifted in the area of healing, some said divinely so. But the break between father and son had been dramatic, and traumatic.

How could the man preach to others to turn away from the evils of drink, Bowen asked himself, only to destroy his own body with it every night? How could he prescribe that cleanliness was next to Godliness when he himself stunk to high heaven for lack of bathing? How could he admonish others to take care of what they had, when he had squandered everything *he* had since Bowen's mother died? "Physician, heal thyself" indeed!

And it wasn't just his father who'd set a bad example. In the process of staying away from his father, he'd spent even more time at school – specifically Harvard University – learning medicine under the tutelage of Drs. George Parkman and John Webster, famous physicians in their own right. So imagine his shock on a morning in November 1849 when he first heard the news that Parkman, who'd almost become a substitute father to him, had disappeared … and then on Thanksgiving Day, watching the police haul away his mentor Webster after charging him with Parkman's murder.

Webster had, indeed, murdered Parkman, after Parkman had demanded Webster pay back some money he owed him. Two great medical men, one dead, the other to be hanged the following year, and all over what? A handful of cash. The scandal made national headlines, and tore apart the city of Boston and the town of Cambridge, where Harvard sat. But it did just as much damage to the heart of the young medical student Bowen Drake.

So while young Bowen did eventually complete his medical studies and earn his M.D. degree – with highest honors, for what little that was worth – he had already rejected even the possibility of practicing medicine. As far as he was concerned, doctoring was nothing but a joke upheld by hypocrites of the worst sort, such as his own father and the late, unlamented John Webster. This son would not be following in his father's footsteps; the student would not pursue the calling of his teachers.

Instead, he'd decided to give his father (and peripherally, his professors) a good dose of his own medicine and do the opposite of everything his father wanted. Maybe that would shock him into reality. Maybe he'd return to being the man he was before the death of Mary Drake, the beloved wife and mother he'd abandoned to the grave.

So after graduation, Bowen took to drinking just like his father. He soon found his sensitive stomach wouldn't last, so he gave it up – but let his father think he hadn't. Games of chance were another option, but after a few weeks in the various gambling hells of the area, he found himself growing bored, not to mention insolvent.

Instead of finding a nice respectable girl to marry, he tried womanizing, but that was even more disastrous. The women kept leaving before Bowen had the chance to break their hearts. Worse yet, they all seemed to wind up with someone perfect for them, get married, and live happily ever after – all while thanking him for his superb matchmaking skills. As far as he knew, he had none – he'd just happen to mention a gentleman he knew, drop a name, and like magic they would show up in town. They'd meet, and off she went. So that was a dead end.

Clearly, he would have to try harder to disappoint his father, punish him for letting his mother die. He hit upon the idea of seeking company of the acutely undesirable – surely that would be enough!

Unfortunately, Bowen's gift for doing good followed him. He headed west and joined an outlaw gang, but within two weeks of joining, half of them came down with a bad case of "the guilts" and turned themselves in! The other half were none too happy to have to disband to save their hides from their blabber-mouthed ex-partners, and correctly blamed Bowen for their plight.

It didn't stop there. He joined another gang and, while trying to rob a train, saved a baby instead. This did nothing to improve his already damaged image in the outlaw world. Nonetheless, Bowen found another gang to hook up with ... but within a month managed to get them all arrested during a stagecoach robbery in which he appeared to save the stagecoach drivers and passengers (one of which was the niece of the owner of the stage line). He even got an honorary mention in the local gazette for his "heroism."

Now brought even lower – and decidedly persona non grata in the criminal community – he figured it couldn't get any worse if he pursued crime as a solo career. Wrong again. His one attempt to rob a bank went awry due to a wagon he'd set aflame as a distraction. Because of a shift in the wind, the local gambling house caught on fire as well, and he wound up on the fire brigade along with everyone else in town. The gambling hell was destroyed, which was a darn shame for the gamblers, but the local Ladies' Society for Godly Living rejoiced that their prayers had been answered and their husbands were now home at night.

So that's where things sat on the third-to-last day of November, the year of Our Lord 1858. Bowen James Drake: frustrated, depressed, unsuccessful at outlawry, with no prospects, no place to go, very few resources and nothing to belong to, not even an outlaw gang.

And to make things worse, he'd heard from an acquaintance back home. Turns out his father had been elated every time he found out about Bowen's heroic exploits – and not only did he let everyone in Philadelphia society know about them, he would get stinking drunk to celebrate. Some of his professors at Harvard, the same ones who had claimed Webster's innocence even as the murderer was led to the gallows, were bragging about their former charge as well.

He'd run as far as he could, as far west as possible to get away from his hypocritical father and the horrendous loss of his mother, from the profession he'd grown to loathe. But he couldn't get away from his special gift, no matter how much he hated it, no matter how little he cared whether he lived or died. Things always worked out for the better where others were concerned when in his company … but they never seemed to work out for him.

He still hated his father for letting his mother die.

He still thought his father was a horrible hypocrite.

He thought medicine was a dodge for charlatans and the two-faced.

He still didn't want anything to do with doctoring as a lifelong vocation.

And he still, just once, would like to see something go *wrong* with everything around him just to let himself know he was "normal," because at this point he was beginning to feel like a freak of nature. He actually even said to *pray* for it to come about.

Obviously, no one had told Bowen the old saying, "be careful what you pray for." Or he just hadn't listened.

That day, Bowen stumbled upon the town of Clear Creek deep in the Oregon Territory – "stumble" being the operative word. Winter had set in, and he was cold, tired, half-starved and even more angry than usual, a nasty combination no matter where a man winds up.

He also had no money, no bullets, and no prospects for getting either.

He reined in his horse at the edge of town and gave the place a once-over. "Good God, where am I?" he mumbled as he stared down the street. He hadn't seen a sign indicating the name of the town when he rode in. In fact, if he didn't know better he'd think the place had appeared out of thin air.

He'd ridden down out of the hills, the last before reaching the rolling prairie, praying his horse would make it through the new-fallen snow without keeling over. The snow had been coming down for days. When it started up again as he reached the prairie he imagined himself frozen to death, his father hearing the news, shaking his head in dismay, and pouring himself a drink. He'd then probably toast his son's cold, dead body and congratulate himself on being such a wonderful father. And the Harvard profs would likely name him a martyr to the cause of medicine he'd so thoroughly rejected.

The mere thought made Bowen seethe. He kept going, if only to keep his father from having one more reason to drink, or his teachers one more reason to brag!

The thought left him as he shook off a jolting chill. He needed to get warm and get his horse taken care of. But how, with no money, with nothing even to trade? He kicked his tired horse forward and continued down the street.

There were no people around and Bowen had to wonder why – it was cold, granted, but not so cold as to shut down business. He passed a mercantile, but it was closed. He noticed a bank and his eyes lit up, but it too was shuttered. "Must be Sunday," he mumbled again as he continued down the street. The bank held promise, so long as he could hold out until it opened – then maybe he could run in and make a forcible "withdrawal." But with no bullets, he'd have to bluff, and that was chancy …

His body stiff and wracked with pain from shivering, he decided first things first, and headed for the livery stable at the end of the street. But when he reached it, there was once again no one about. He unsaddled his horse anyway, put it in a stall and fed it. The only other occupant was a huge draft horse that eyed him suspiciously as he went about his work. He ignored the horse as best he could but had the uncanny feeling the beast was watching his every move. At one point he stared at it, and it stared right back until he looked away.

The thought that a horse had just beat him at a staring contest only made him angrier. He grumbled, shook off another series of chills, and left the livery stable. He'd have to figure out some way to get his horse out before anyone wanted money. If he wasn't so cold and hungry, he'd be able to think better, but the lack of food had muddled his mind and there was nothing to eat in the livery except hay …

For the first time, he noticed the church building off by itself, about a hundred yards away. Wagons were parked outside, along with various individuals' horses. Sunday, sure enough.

Bowen glanced toward the livery, then back at the horses tied to the church's hitching post. Hmmm …

A sudden blast of wind caught his hat and blew it right off his head, forcing him to chase after it. It was becoming even colder, and he wondered if he was going to be able to make it through the day. His hands and feet had gone numb, and if he didn't get in out of the wind he wasn't going to be in any shape to rob the bank, or anything else for that matter.

But his new idea seemed to warm him. Maybe he could take advantage of the entire town's church attendance, rob the bank now, and hightail it out of there on a fresh horse swiped from the church's hitching post … that might work. But other thoughts started to crowd in: his mother's favorite shawl, the song she used to play on the piano when they had company over, her cherry pies, the whiff of lilac he'd get whenever she gave him a hug as a child …

He didn't remember falling, yet here he was lying in the snow, his head swimming with memories of his dead mother and good-for-nothing father. Warmth began to seep into his bones, or was it something else? And was that an angel staring down at him? Oh, God, had he gone and let himself freeze to death? Had it finally come to this? Turned into an icicle in a nothing town out in the middle of the Oregon Territory where no one knew him? Worse yet, would his father never know of his passing? To die and not be able to strike that final blow to the man stung as badly as the cold had …

But Bowen didn't want to think anymore. In fact, he couldn't. Everything, inside his mind and out, had gone black.

"Grandpa! I think he's dead!" Elsie Waller cried in dismay as she looked at the man lying in the snow. She'd spied him as she made her trek back to her grandparents' house. She'd only arrived yesterday, and already she was staring into the face of tragedy? However, the sort of tragedy she was familiar with certainly didn't look like this. The man lying before her had to be the handsomest she'd ever seen.

Grandpa Waller (in actuality her third cousin on her father's side, but he insisted she call him Grandpa) bent to the still form and checked for a pulse. "He's alive! Some of you help me get him up, will you?" he shouted to several men now running toward them.

"Good Lord!" Harrison Cooke exclaimed. "Doc, what happened?"

"My guess is he's frozen half to death," Grandpa commented sarcastically. "Let's get him over to the saloon!"

Elsie watched as two of the Cooke brothers, Harrison and Colin, picked the man up and started to drag him toward Mulligan's Saloon. The tips of his boots left two funny tracks in the snow as she followed them a few feet behind.

They reached the saloon and the men carried the body inside, where Grandpa had them prop him up in a chair. "Someone get me some hot coffee for this man! Elsie, come here."

She went to where Harrison and Colin held the unconscious man up in a sitting position. His lips were blue and looked odd against the dark stubble of his jaw. To Elsie, he looked very dead. But if Grandpa said he wasn't, he surely wasn't.

"Run upstairs, honey, and fetch me some blankets," Grandpa Waller told her. "Don't worry, the door'll be unlocked and Mrs. Mulligan won't mind. Now hurry!"

Elsie ran as fast as she could. She'd been in the Mulligans' parlor yesterday afternoon when Mrs. Mulligan had greeted her, along with Grandpa and Grandma, when she'd gotten off the stage. They'd gone to the saloon for tea and some leftover cake from a huge Thanksgiving celebration and wedding a few days before. She'd met Mr. Mulligan too, and the Dunnigans who owned the mercantile in town.

She pushed the thoughts aside as she burst into the upper rooms of the saloon and went straight for the quilt folded up on a rocking chair. Mrs. Mulligan had told her how she liked to put the quilt over her while she knitted in the evenings. Snatching it up, she pelted back down the stairs.

She put it in her grandfather's outstretched hand and watched as he placed it over the man's shoulders. "Come around here, Elsie," he told her as Harrison tucked the quilt in between the man's body and the chair to hold it in place.

Elsie did as she was told and stood in front of her grandfather's patient.

"Grab a chair and pull it alongside this fella," Grandpa Waller instructed. "Try to rub some feeling back into his hands. Colin, where's that coffee?"

Colin Cooke came running from the kitchen area of the saloon. "Thank Heaven Mary had a pot on the stove!" He handed the cup to her grandfather as she grabbed a chair, sat and picked up one of the man's ice-cold hands. They, too, were bluish, though not as bad as the man's lips. She started to rub the hand vigorously as she watched for any sign of life. There was none.

She felt tears prick the backs of her eyes, and wondered why she was having such a strong reaction. She didn't know this man, had never seen him. Yet his face was so handsome, so strong. What a shame to lose one's life to the cold and elements so young. Sure, he was probably older than she was, but still younger than most.

In fact, he was probably about Harrison Cooke's age – and Harrison, according to Mrs. Mulligan, was twenty-five going on twenty-six come Christmas, with his first child on the way. Of course, Mrs. Mulligan needn't have told her the last part; Harrison himself made sure of that!

It had been one of the first things out of his mouth when she was introduced to him that morning in church. "Hello!" he'd exclaimed when Grandma made the introductions. "I'm going to have a baby! Isn't it wonderful?" She hadn't even met his wife yet!

Elsie had tried not to laugh, but failed miserably. It was the way he said it – the Cooke brothers were English and had charming accents. But Harrison's sudden blurt about having a baby seemed so out of character for an Englishman. It may have been impolite of her, and was almost certainly improper, but it was the first time she'd laughed in the four months since her Grandpa Teddy (her real grandfather, not a third cousin) had died. She'd needed that.

Maybe that's why the sight of the near-lifeless man stirred her so. Her emotions were positively raw.

The hand she held suddenly gripped her own. "Oh!" she cried. "Grandpa!"

The man's eyes opened wide. He looked at her and squeezed her hand tighter. "Where am I?" he rasped.

"Take it easy, old chap," Harrison said as he came around the chair to stand before him. "It looks like you've had a rough time of it. We need to get you warm."

Grandpa Waller came out from the kitchen. "Give him some coffee, then bring him in here! Should have thought to have you do that in the first place!"

Harrison handed the man a cup but he only stared at it.

"It's warm," Elsie assured him. "Please drink it. You have to get better!"

He looked at her. Chocolate-brown eyes met her blue ones and locked. His were sad, full of regret, while hers were full of wonder. "Please," she urged.

He raised the hand she'd been rubbing and tried to hold the cup, but couldn't manage it. She took it from

Harrison and held it to his lips for him. He looked at her for a moment as if he wasn't quite sure what she was doing, but finally put his icy hands over her warm ones and brought the cup the rest of the way. He drank slowly at first, then a bit more greedily.

"Careful now," she warned. "It's hot."

"Not that hot," Harrison corrected. "Just warm. But that's what's important."

Hot or not, the man drained it, took the cup from his lips and started to shiver fiercely.

"We've got to get him into the kitchen, like Grandpa said." Elsie urged.

"Right you are," Harrison agreed. Colin stepped out of the back of the saloon and together, he and Harrison got the man up out of the chair and half-dragged him to the kitchen. Tears began to fall unbidden as Elsie trailed along behind them. The poor man couldn't even walk!

They sat him in a chair that Grandpa Waller had placed near the cookstove. Harrison readjusted the quilt around him, then bent to take off the man's boots. The man didn't argue as Harrison and Colin both started to rub his cold feet. He had no socks, only the boots, and Elsie tried to imagine what it would feel like to be so cold, her feet all but frozen. She nearly cried out with the image it evoked in her mind's eye, and immediately went to the coffee pot to get him another cup.

"Good idea, Elsie; get some more coffee down him!"

"Tip in a little whiskey – this poor things needs some antifreeze," Grandma added as she rushed into the kitchen, handing a bottle off to Elsie. "Land sakes, what happened? Who is he?"

"No idea - found him passed out in the snow," Grandpa told her.

"Oh, my Lord!"

"We'll treat him here. No room at our place with Elsie there now," he told her.

Elsie winced in guilt as she brought the man another cup of coffee, this one laced with some of the cheap stuff from Mulligan's well-stocked bar. She realized she had the only extra bedroom in the Wallers' home, but didn't know they used it as a patient room. Now she did, of course …

She offered the cup to the man, but his hands were shaking so badly he couldn't hold it himself. "Let me help you," she told him in a soft voice. She placed one of his hands on the cup, then the other, and put her own over them. She knew the warmth from the cup would help his hands thaw from the bitter cold.

He looked at her gratefully and raised the cup to his lips once more. Standing before him, she helped him to sip the contents. "What's your name?" she asked gently.

He lowered the cup, looked her in the eye and said, "Bo … Bowen … Bowen D-D-D-Drake."

She let go of the breath she'd been holding and smiled at him. "I'm Elsie Waller. Welcome to Clear Creek, Mr. Drake."

Two

SHE WAS BEAUTIFUL … THE most beautiful woman Bowen had ever seen, and he'd seen his share. Her hair was a light golden brown, her eyes deep blue. She had high cheekbones and a Cupid's-bow mouth that at the moment was parted as if for a kiss. She was wearing a simple brown calico dress, the hem of which was wet from walking through the snow.

He briefly wondered if this was the same face he'd seen when he'd thought he was dead. He'd had a sense of being carried or dragged through the snow, then nothing but slivers of light coming and going and the sensation of needles stabbing him all over.

He focused on her, this beautiful creature standing before him, to keep from crying out. She still held her hands over his, and it was pure Heaven to have them sandwiched between the warm cup and her soft skin. "Thank you," he managed to whisper as his body convulsed with shivering. "I … I owe you my life."

"Well now, son, Elsie may have found ya, but was Harrison and Colin that brought you in here," an elderly man told him.

One of the men looked up from his ministrations to Bowen's feet. "Harrison Cooke, at your service. But let's don't make this a habit."

"Quite right," the other man said. "I can never get him to do this for me at home!"

Bowen managed a weak chuckle amidst the shivers,

then took a second look at the men at his feet. They sounded English.

"I'm Colin Cooke. I'd shake your hand but mine are a bit full at the moment."

Yes, definitely English, Bowen thought.

"That should be enough, boys. Cover him up good now," the elderly man told them.

The old woman who had come in earlier handed them her shawl as another couple entered the kitchen. "Good heavens!" one of them, a middle-aged woman, exclaimed. "What's happened?"

"Mr. Drake," Harrison Cooke said. "May I introduce you to Mr. and Mrs. Patrick Mulligan, the proprietors of the establishment in which you now find yourself."

He wanted to hold out his hand to Mr. Mulligan, but the thought of letting go of the warm cup – or removing his hands from the young woman's – was too much to bear. He offered a smile instead as he once again shivered violently. At least it seemed to be less dramatic now.

"Grandpa," the beauty said. "Isn't there any more we can do for him?" She looked down at Bowen, her blue eyes full of emotion, and he melted. It was as if she could thaw the darkest, coldest part of his heart.

He closed his eyes against her power, her nearness. His hatred for his father, and to a lesser extent his professors, was all that had kept him going, kept him alive these past months. He couldn't afford to let the girl affect him like this. If he lost it, he would surely die out in this wilderness. He'd need his anger for when he moved on.

But *when* could he move on? He had no money, no prospects, no supplies except his horse. Heck, right now he didn't even have his horse! Or his boots – where did they go? He'd seen them only a moment before, but now they'd disappeared …

Just then, Colin Cooke wrapped his feet in the woman's warm shawl, and Bowen felt his eyes roll back in his head in pleasure. He could ... he could worry about the other ... things later ...

"You must be hungry," said the beautiful girl – Elsie, was it? She let go of his hands, went to the stove, picked up a ladle from a worktable and peeked into a large pot that had been shoved to one side of the stove top. Upon lifting the lid, the smell of stew reached his nose and made his mouth water. His stomach growled loudly.

The girl turned and smiled at him. "Mrs. Mulligan, may I give him some of this?"

"Of course, girl. You don't need to ask. Mrs. Dunnigan won't mind at all."

Elsie looked at him and smiled again. "I'm sure you'll like Mrs. Dunnigan's cooking. I hear she's famous in these parts for it."

"Among other things," Colin Cooke mumbled under his breath, then replied, "good idea, Miss Elsie. Let's give him a spot of stew; that should set him right!" He crossed to the other side of the kitchen and fetched a bowl from a cupboard, handing it to the smiling girl.

She dished up a bowl for Bowen and offered it to him, but his hands had begun to shake again. Of all the times – he wouldn't even be able to feed himself!

He glanced up helplessly at her as she took the coffee cup from him, set it aside, then pulled a chair up next to him. Good grief! Was she going to do what he thought she was?

She smiled again, dipped the spoon into the bowl, and held it out to him.

The humiliation! Why couldn't he get his hands to stop shaking? But the stew smelled so good ... *Oh, Bowen, forget about your pride and eat something!* He looked at her, swallowed hard, and opened his mouth.

She very gently put the spoon in his mouth. He watched breathlessly as the blue of her eyes grew darker when she leaned toward him. The stew was incredible, her skin even more so now that she was close enough for him to get a good look at her. It was creamy and perfect; her dark lashes long and lush, the kind women grew jealous of. Her hair was thick, plaited and piled atop her head, and he wondered how long it would be if she were to let it fall from its pins. Her dress was simple, but she filled it out well – *very* well, to the point that he caught himself staring at areas of her anatomy he shouldn't be.

She blushed and gave him another bite of stew. He took it and reveled in the food's warmth as it traveled down to his gut to settle there, much the same way the girl in front of him was making other parts of him warm. Not physically, but some other way he couldn't put his finger on. He'd never felt this before, and he wondered what it could be. It was like heat emanating from somewhere deep inside of him.

"Would you like some more?" she asked in a soft, delicate voice.

He stared at her, then looked at the bowl in her hand. The stew was gone. He hadn't realized he'd eaten it all.

"If he can handle it, give him some more," the older man, Grandpa, told her. "Otherwise he needs to finish warming up,"

She nodded at him, then gave her attention back to Bowen. "I can get you another portion if you'd like."

He nodded, too dumbstruck at that moment to say anything. She was so pretty, all creamy skin and curves. Maybe he *should* hang around awhile …

"So, this here's the fella, eh?" a man's voice said from behind him.

Bowen tried to turn in the chair but found it took more effort than he could manage.

The man walked around to in front of him. "I'm Sheriff Hughes, son."

Bowen froze. Sheriff? This place actually had a sheriff? *Uh-oh...*

"Harrison here tells me they found you just before you decided to take a little winter nap."

Bowen looked up at him. He was middle-aged, with salt-and-pepper hair. "I'm grateful they did."

"Trust me when I tell ya, you couldn't have been found by finer folk," the sheriff told him. "But what I want to know is what in Sam blazes you were doing crossing the prairie in this kind of weather by yourself? Are you plumb loco?"

Bowen inwardly groaned. What was he to tell them? He couldn't very well tell them he'd been kicked out of yet another outlaw gang. "Had some trouble on the trail and got separated from my party." It wasn't entirely untrue. The last gang he was with had tied him to a tree and ridden off without him. He'd been lucky to get himself free before he froze to death. But at the time, that was the least of his worries. The dirty scoundrels took his money, emptied his guns of bullets and only left him his horse because they figured the animal wasn't worth enough to take along with them.

"Well, it looks like your luck's changed, son," the sheriff told him. "Let's hope it gets better from here on out. You let me know if you need anything."

"Actually ..." Bowen said. He couldn't believe he was going to ask this. "You wouldn't happen to know if anyone around here has some work that needs doing, would you?"

"Work?" the sheriff asked. "What kind?"

Bowen swallowed hard. All eyes were on him at this point. "Ah … well … seeing as how the weather looks like it's settled in for a spell, I thought I'd stick around. That being the case, I'd need to … to earn my keep."

"That's understandable, but it don't answer my question. What kind of work?"

Bowen looked at the different faces staring at him: the elderly gentleman and his wife, the saloon owners, the English brothers, and finally the vision of loveliness sitting in the chair next to him. "Ah … anything, actually." Good grief, what was he doing? But he knew the bad weather wasn't going to let him leave even with a good horse and provisions, of which he had neither. What choice did he have?

The sheriff scratched his head. "Not sure, son. I'll send Cyrus Van Cleet over. He's building the hotel and could probably use an extra pair of hands. You skilled at anything special?"

Bowen's chest tightened and he closed his eyes. *No, no, no! I won't!* "Nothing special," he finally replied. "But I can swing a hammer as good as anyone else, I reckon."

"Well, that should suit Cyrus just fine. I'll try to catch him before he leaves for home. He's over at the hotel now." The sheriff put on his hat and left.

Everyone watched him go before Grandpa started to poke and prod at Bowen. "You'd best stick close to this here stove for a while, son. Get yourself warmed up real good." He turned to Mr. Mulligan. "You don't mind, do ya?"

Mr. Mulligan looked Bowen over carefully. "No, he can stay here until Cyrus figures out what to do with him," he replied in an Irish brogue. "If he stays on, I'm sure he'll be bunking over at the hotel with the rest of the men."

Colin Cooke stepped forward. He'd been standing off to one side of the stove since the sheriff arrived. "I say, I'm sure Cyrus will have something for you. But if not, you could also stay at the livery stable. It's not much, but there's a small stove and a cot to sleep on."

"M-much obliged," Bowen said, then looked at each person in the room. "To all of you. You've shown me great kindness." Guilt suddenly assailed him. These people *had* shown him great kindness – and here he'd been trying to figure out how to rob them blind!

"Are ya good with your hands, son?" Grandpa asked. "They're working on the interior of the hotel this winter, making it nice and fancy. I know they could use someone good with their hands."

Bowen stared at him. Yes, he *was* good with his hands, but he didn't want to have anything to do with doctoring, not if he could help it!

"I'm sorry," the man added. "I guess in all the excitement, I forgot to introduce myself. I'm Doc Waller and that there's Sarah, my wife."

"But you can call me Grandma. Everyone around these parts does," the old woman said.

"And this here is Elsie – she's come to live with us. Arrived just yesterday, in fact. Come all the way from Nowhere."

"Nowhere?"

"It's up in the Washington Territory."

Bowen looked from one face to the other. "I'm sorry, but who calls a town Nowhere?"

"Well, ya see, my cousin Teddy and his friend Frank headed out west together, and when they got to …"

"Not now, Doc!" Grandma Waller interrupted. "We got things to do, remember? If Mr. Drake is warming up, then we'd best get on out to the Turners' place and check on Tommy."

Doc nodded and turned back to Bowen. "Young Tommy Turner fell out of the hayloft day after Thanksgiving and got himself banged up pretty good. I told his father I'd come by and check on him after church. I'd best get on then."

"I'll come with you, Doc." Colin offered.

"Why, thank you, Colin. I think I'll let you do that." He turned to Grandma. "Why don't you take Elsie on home? No sense in both of us going out to the Turners' place if Colin's gonna tag along."

Grandma nodded, then looked at Bowen's feet. "Of course, this means I'm gonna need my shawl back, Mr. Drake."

He looked at the brown shawl she'd wrapped around his feet earlier. "I thank you for lending it to me. That was very kind." He then looked at Elsie and felt his breath hitch. "And ... and thank you, too. For ... everything." He couldn't bring himself to say *thank you for feeding me.* He felt helpless enough as it was.

She blushed and smiled. "You're welcome, Mr. Drake. I hope you'll be staying on."

He lifted a brow at that.

"I ... I mean, until you're fully recovered," she quickly added. "I'm sure you'll be fine in no time ... but ... Mr. Van Cleet might need your help."

Hmmm, did this wondrous creature *want* him to stay? Or was propriety governing her quick response? Judging by her blush, it wasn't just politeness. "I look forward to speaking with him," he said.

She quickly turned and stepped toward Grandma Waller, then faced him again. Her smile was brilliant, and he felt its warmth seep into his bones. Of course he knew that wasn't possible – he was, by training at least, a man of science – but there was no other way to describe how it made him feel. He was beginning to consider staying in Clear Creek simply to see if the sensation could be repeated.

"One of us will be sure to check on you later, son," Doc Waller said. "Until then, you stay here and speak to Mr. Van Cleet when he comes, see what he says."

"I'll do that," Bowen said, never taking his eyes from the picture of perfection standing next to the doctor's wife. "I don't believe I fancy going anywhere for a while."

Doc Waller glanced from Bowen to Elsie and back again. "Yeah, I can see that," he chuckled under his breath. Then he motioned to Colin Cooke, and together they left the saloon.

Three

ELSIE BLUSHED, AND BLUSHED, AND blushed some more. She was glad for the wind whipping against her as she and Grandma Waller trudged back to the house. People would at least assume that the chill was the cause of her red face!

What had she been thinking, telling a stranger she hoped he'd stay in town? For Heaven's sake, she was a stranger here herself for the most part! She hadn't even been in Clear Creek twenty-four hours, and she'd already embarrassed herself and acted like a … a … well, not a lady, that was for sure!

"When we get back to the house, I want you to start on the rolls for supper," Grandma yelled over the wind. "Land sakes, I may have to rest my bones awhile. Can you manage things for me, child?"

"Of course, Grandma. Are you really that tired?" Elsie asked as they stepped up onto the front porch of the Wallers' home.

"It must be the cold. Seems every year I get a little achier in places I didn't think one could ache!"

They went inside and Elsie followed Grandma Waller down the hall to the kitchen, where she immediately tended the stove. She put on a kettle for tea, then showed Elsie where everything was that she would need in order to make the rolls. A large pot of soup was already simmering on the stove – Grandma had started it that morning. "This is the same recipe your Aunt Mabel always used. I'm sure you're familiar with it," Grandma said as she handed Elsie a worn piece of paper with a recipe scrawled on it.

"If it's Aunt Mabel's recipe then I don't need to look at it – I have it memorized!" Elsie said proudly.

"Well, look at you then, memorizing your Aunt Mabel's recipes! Good for you, child – I know these rolls will turn out just fine! Do you know her recipe for peach pie?"

"Yes, ma'am."

"Well, well, that's just fine! I lost it years ago and that darn woman never did give it up to me! I thought she'd take it to her grave and I'd never get to taste that sweet peach pie of hers again! Ha! You be sure and write it down for me, child, ya hear?"

Elsie laughed. She was quickly growing to love Grandma and Grandpa Waller. True, she hadn't seen them in years, but she had nothing but fond memories of the couple – including how feisty Grandma Waller could be! "I'll do that, but first I think I'd better take care of these rolls and get them in the oven."

"You go right ahead," Grandma said, then yawned. "I think I'll go upstairs and lie down a few minutes. That cold wind takes the fight right out of me!" She kissed Elsie on the forehead, then went down the hall and up the stairs to her room.

Elsie watched her go, then took off her shawl, hung it up, and put on an apron. She mixed the ingredients she needed, formed her dough, put it in a bowl, and covered it to let it rise. Once that was done, she made herself a quick cup of tea, and sat at the kitchen table to contemplate the events of the day.

Correction … make that the events of the past two years.

Poor Grandpa Teddy. How she missed him. He'd been the light in her dark world for a long time, and Elsie couldn't imagine life without him. Until his death several months ago gave her no choice. She'd been so busy since that she hadn't had much time to cry.

Grandpa Teddy's lawyer wanted to put things in order right away, and that included shipping her off to Clear Creek just as soon as he was able. Now here she was, at this table, with this cup of tea, wondering about that handsome stranger she'd found in the snow.

Her heart had leaped in her chest at the sight of him, her eyes automatically searching the ground for blood. But there was none she could see, and she'd quickly pondered what could have happened to him as she approached the still form. That is, until she noticed the blue lips and realized that he was freezing to death. He looked already dead, and her relief at discovering he was still alive astounded even her. But she had no wish to see such a young, strong-looking man lose his life to the elements.

She was curious as to how he came to be in such an unfortunate state in the first place. Everyone knew how dangerous it was to travel alone in this kind of weather. A snowfall could start out small, but soon turn into a whiteout. She'd seen it happen plenty of times back in Nowhere and, even though Clear Creek was more than two hundred miles to the south, the weather, for the most part, was pretty much the same.

"Bowen Drake," she whispered as she remembered the way his large hands covered hers as she held the warm cup to his lips. She sighed at the thought. It didn't matter that so far she'd only seen him flat on his back, in a chair, or dragged by two men; she could still imagine him standing and yes, he would be quite tall – at least as tall as the Cooke brothers. Well, the two she'd met, Colin and Harrison. She hadn't seen the eldest, Duncan, but he was supposed to be the tallest and handsomest of the three. And a real English duke besides!

Elsie smiled at the thought. Grandma Waller had barely stopped talking since she got off the stage the day before, but all the information was useful. She had spent the time explaining who was who and what was what, so Elsie wouldn't get confused later. A good thing, too – if she hadn't known that Clear Creek was home to a duke, his duchess, and a real live princess, she never would have believed it!

According to Grandma, Duncan Cooke had inherited the Stantham estate and title only months before. He and his wife, Cozette – who was French (sort of) – were leaving for London in the early spring. Meanwhile, a woman and her daughter had come to town about the time Duncan and Cozette were courting, and the woman, a Mrs. Van Zuyen, had been married to a prince! According to Grandma, she was a countess before she was married and after the prince met with an untimely tragedy (which left his wife and daughter alone in the world) became the countess once again.

Her daughter, on the other hand, as daughter of the prince, was next in line to the throne. Elsie had yet to hear the full tale – there hadn't been time since her arrival for Grandma to tell her all of it. She did know the daughter ... what was her name, Mary? Mattie? ... she married the town blacksmith, who really wasn't a blacksmith at all.

She had to take another sip of tea. It was all so confusing, yet so wonderfully exciting! Who would have ever imagined a little town like Clear Creek could be home to so much European royalty? Not for much longer, however – all of them would be leaving in the spring to take care of business across the sea.

Elsie sighed. Just when she arrived, too! How much adventure had she missed already?

But … not even royalty could compare with the smoldering brown eyes of Bowen Drake. She had been thinking about the crowned heads of Clear Creek to keep from thinking about Mr. Drake, but her mind kept wandering back to him! And yet, how could she not think of him after the way he'd been looking at her earlier? How could she ever forget the feel of his hands over her own, or the smell of snow and pine that clung to his hair and clothes?

Elsie sighed again and stared into her teacup. What did it matter? He probably didn't think twice about it. The smoldering of his eyes was more than likely caused by the hot coffee and Mrs. Dunnigan's stew, not by the sight of her. He had been freezing to death, after all.

Another sip. She wondered what would happen to the handsome stranger now that he was here. She was as much a stranger in town as he was, but she at least had a place to call home. And she had to admit, she was looking forward to the change. The town of Nowhere had been exactly that: *nowhere*. It was even smaller than Clear Creek (no mean feat) and surrounded by an ever-increasing number of apple orchards. A fine thing if you were an apple farmer. When you were a young woman of marrying age, and every man for miles around was either chained to his farm, his father's farm, or running off to Oregon City or Seattle to seek his fortune, well … that wasn't so fine.

Of course, there were the Riley brothers, Clayton and Spencer; they were both pretty handsome … for a couple of teenage boys. Elsie didn't fancy waiting around for them to grow up. Besides, she'd be considered an old maid by then, even if Clayton was only three years younger than she was! It didn't help that that busybody Nellie Davis was telling everyone for miles around that her daughter Charlotte would marry Clayton as soon as they were of age.

She smiled to herself. Apparently Nellie hadn't told Clayton – and it was also common knowledge that Clayton couldn't stand Charlotte! (And didn't think much of her mother either, to tell the truth.)

Elsie giggled and thanked Heaven above that no one was trying to marry her off or choose a man for her. She had her own mind and her own goals, and she knew that here in Clear Creek she'd see them fulfilled. Already she'd found a man she thought interesting. Too bad she didn't know if he felt the same way about her – or could even feel his toes, for that matter.

She set down her cup and went to check the dough. "Well, Mr. Drake," she said to herself as she punched down the slowly-rising mass, "I'm sure if you spent some time with me, you'd find me quite interesting."

Of course, that was it! All she had to do was spend time with Bowen and she was sure he'd like what he saw. Maybe even enough to stay! And he *had* mentioned he needed someplace to winter, hadn't he? Or had she been the one who'd brought that up? But no matter – he would need to find a place to winter, and couldn't possibly make it to Oregon City on his own, not at this time of year. Grandpa Waller had told her the last of the supply wagons had come and gone, and it would be months before more came to town.

Elsie smiled. "Well, Mr. Drake, it looks like you'll have to stay on after all." She punched down the dough again, pleased with the thought. Now all she had to do was make sure he did. Then there'd be plenty of time for him to discover just how interesting she could be.

Of course, this meant that she'd have to come up with a good reason to spend time with the mysterious man. Hmmm … now what good reason was there?

"Blast this play!" the Rev. Josiah King grumbled as he scratched out the lines he'd just written and ran a hand through his hair. "I can't come up with any good ideas!"

His new wife, Annie, wrapped her arms around him from behind the chair and kissed his hair. "You're trying too hard. Slow down; relax. Let's have some coffee and talk about it. Maybe we should stick to something more traditional."

Josiah let go a heavy sigh. "Traditional. Perfect. That will please everybody, I'm sure." He turned in his chair to look at her. "You know the whole town wants to do the Christmas story. But I think we should do something different."

"Maybe they all want the Christmas story because they already know it. It doesn't scare them."

"What do you mean, scare them?"

Annie shrugged. "The townspeople are familiar with it. I doubt any of them are used to getting up and performing in front of a crowd. It would be the easiest thing for them to do."

Josiah blew his hair off his forehead. "I see your point. Maybe we should stick with the basics."

"You could always make it a little different. Add your own twist to it."

He eyed his wife. She was clever, and her suggestion made him smile. "Why, Mrs. King, I do believe you've struck upon something."

"And don't you want this Christmas to be memorable for the people leaving town in the spring – the Cookes, the Dupries, the Bergs?"

He took one of her hands, guided her around the chair, then pulled her into his lap. "You never cease to amaze me, Mrs. King." He bent his face to hers and kissed her soundly.

When he finally broke the kiss, she looked up at him, her eyes shining. "Besides, Reverend King, don't you think it would be fun to see those families performing for the townsfolk? After all, they're the ones who are going to have to get used to being in front of crowds."

"Good grief, I hadn't thought of that! Why, we might be doing them a favor casting them in our play!"

"And with the Christmas story, there'll be plenty of other parts to go around. Just think of all those animals in the stable, the innkeeper, the three wise men…"

Josiah finally conceded. "All right. We'll do it. The Christmas story it is. But you're still going to help me write it."

Annie smiled. "Of course. We'll also need costumes, a makeshift stable …"

"Whoa! Slow down, we haven't written it yet! How do you know what we'll need?"

She shrugged again. "It's the Christmas story. Everyone knows what's needed to perform that."

"What happened to adding my own twist? Maybe I don't want the wise men to ride in on camels – maybe I want them to ride in on … on pumpkins!"

Annie's face screwed up at him. "Pumpkins?"

Josiah laughed, kissed his wife, then lifted her out of his lap and stood. "Right now I want some pumpkin pie if there's any left. Then I'll write the play. With luck, we can hold auditions this week and next Sunday after church."

"There's pie left, and don't worry, I'll help you. But I think you'd better leave the pumpkins out of it. Somehow I can't picture Duncan Cooke dressed up as a pumpkin."

Josiah laughed at that. "Nor can I ... well, maybe I can. I've known the Cookes longer than you have. I'm sure we can work this out so the entire town can get involved, but not have everyone actually in the play. I'll write up an announcement and post it at the mercantile."

"Perfect. That will give us both enough time to, ah, brace ourselves."

Josiah quickly nodded his agreement. He knew as well as his wife that the town was already abuzz at the prospect of having the first Christmas play performed in Clear Creek. In fact, it was the first play, period, and most folks fancied a part for themselves. The Rev. King only hoped that once everything was set, there'd still be enough people left over to be in the audience!

Four

"WHAT'S AN EDUCATED MAN LIKE you doing out here in Clear Creek?" Cyrus Van Cleet wasn't the sort to beat around the bush. In fact, Bowen was still trying to figure out how the wiry little man had wheedled the information out of him so effortlessly.

It was probably because Mr. Van Cleet had a calming quality to him that made Bowen think of warm sunshine on fall-colored leaves. It was almost as if the man could bring him back to a place in his childhood, one unfettered with his father's constant drinking, his professors' platitudes and his own constant running. Talking with him was effortless.

"I wanted to come west and see what it was like," Bowen told him. "I guess all that education didn't do me much good on the trail. I almost killed myself several times over just getting here."

Mr. Van Cleet wrinkled his nose. "You're plumb lucky you didn't freeze to death. Happens all the time in these parts." He released a long sigh. "Well, I could certainly use a man like you. I've got myself a bookkeeper already, so that's out. Let me see …"

Bowen battled the last bouts of cold running through him as he watched the man decide. He'd thawed out as best he could before Mr. Mulligan led him to the half- finished hotel where Mr. Van Cleet was giving instructions to his foreman, a man named August Bennett. If anyone knew how tough it would be trying to get from Clear Creek to Oregon City at this time of year, it would be him. Mr. Van Cleet explained to Bowen that August had made the trip many times, being in charge of the supply wagons for the hotel. Now that winter was setting in, he'd remain in Clear Creek until it was safe enough to make another run – and that wouldn't be for months.

"I suppose August could use an assistant. You knowing how to read and write as well as you do would help. Mrs. Hansen – that's the bookkeeper I mentioned – is in charge of payroll, but August will need someone to help him with inventory, make sure there's no theft, that sort of thing."

Bowen felt a sudden surge of heat and hoped nothing showed on his face. "Theft?"

"Oh small things, really – sometimes a hammer or a saw will go missing. They usually show up a few days later, but you never know."

Bowen nodded and swallowed hard. "Yes, you never know …," he hastily agreed.

"You can start tomorrow. In fact, why don't you bunk with August? He's got a room up on the second floor – it's one of the few with all four walls up!"

Bowen chuckled and automatically scanned the unfinished lobby of the hotel for August Bennett, but he was nowhere to be seen.

"Follow me – I'll show you the room, not that it's hard to find!" Cyrus laughed and motioned him toward the stairs. "Just got these put in," he said, patting the banister. "Much nicer than ladders."

Bowen followed him up the stairs and turned left down a hall. A balustrade was on his left, hotel rooms on his right. Some of the rooms had been walled in, but most were only framed. The upper landing they traversed ended and turned into another hall, with rooms on either side. Mr. Van Cleet went straight to the door at the end of it and knocked.

The door opened. August Bennett pulled up a pair of suspenders and yawned. "Mr. Van Cleet! Did you need something? I was just going to take a little nap."

"Oh, so sorry to disturb you, August, but I though Mr. Drake could bunk with you. I've decided to hire him on as … well, as your assistant."

August raised his brow and looked Bowen over a moment before he returned his attention to Mr. Van Cleet. "I need an assistant?"

"Well, we can't expect him to go on to Oregon City in this weather, and certainly not alone. He's an educated man, and can help you keep track of the inventory and supplies while you keep track of the workers. You might as well get to know each other if you're going to work together, so here we are."

August again looked Bowen up and down.

"I believe Mr. Bennett knows if he would benefit from one such as me, Mr. Van Cleet," Bowen told him. "Or if not."

Mr. Van Cleet looked between the two men. "Well, August? Think you can use him?"

August looked – and sounded – skeptical. "You ever been in closed quarters with a bunch of men during winter?"

Bowen eyed him and tried not to smile. If they only knew … "Yes, sir, I have."

"These men have had the freedom that comes with sunshine and warm weather, Mr. Drake. But over the next few months, they're gonna be pent up here in the evenings or down at the saloon. Men can get pretty cranky when cabin fever sets in."

"I understand, Mr. Bennett." Bowen answered, wondering where this was going.

"There *is* something you can do, now that I think of it. I'll be too busy and, with Mr. Berg not coming into town as often with winter setting in, we'll need someone to remind the men to mind their manners."

Now Bowen was confused. "Manners?" he said. "And … who is Mr. Berg?"

August smiled. "You haven't been here long enough to notice yet, but there's a definite lack of females in this town."

Bowen thought a moment. He'd met at least three – four if he counted the heavy, crotchety woman who'd stormed into the kitchen of the saloon, snatched up a ladle and started to wave it about like a weapon. He didn't catch her name and didn't care to – he just didn't want to cross paths with her again if he could help it! "What does that have to do with me?"

"Well, Doc and Grandma have one of Doc's relations living with them now – she just got into town yesterday. Only a matter of time before the men start to look for excuses to run to Doc to be tended to for the slightest thing just to get a look at her."

"Elsie?" Bowen gasped.

August smiled. "You've met her."

"She … she found me."

August exchanged a quick glance with Mr. Van Cleet. "Then you see my point."

The thought of the workers swarming the Wallers' house sent an unfamiliar fury through Bowen. He had a vision of them trying to break down the door to get to the beautiful girl inside, the one who'd brought him back to the living and helped him thaw out. Her soft skin, her fresh scent, those beautiful blue eyes … the memory of them hit hard and fast. No wonder August was concerned. "Yes, I see your point," Bowen finally said.

"They'll need to be reminded, and you'll need to keep an eye out for her. If the men so much as spy her walking to the mercantile, they'll stop working and try to find some excuse to go shopping."

Bowen stared at him and nodded. "So what do you want me to do?"

"I'm sure Mr. Van Cleet will agree with me, but I think it would be best that you accompany Miss Elsie any time she's out and about. The men will be less likely to go looking for reasons to quit working if they see she's with someone. I don't have the time, but you ... well, there are only so many things you can count and keep track of, Mr. Drake."

Play escort to that exquisite creature? Accompany her through town whenever she set foot outside her door? Protect her in general? Perhaps staying in Clear Creek wouldn't be so bad after all! And it would help pass the time until he decided when and how to leave town with more than he'd arrived with. *Much* more. "I'll see to it she's not disturbed by the men, and doesn't become a distraction."

"I agree wholeheartedly!" Mr. Van Cleet said. "I'll let Doc and Grandma know. Oh, and Mr. Drake? Might I add that if you yourself become too distracted with her, you too might be paid a visit by Mr. Berg." They both chuckled.

Bowen looked from one face to the other. "Who *is* this Mr. Berg?"

"Let us just say a run-in with Mr. Berg is not something you want," August explained. "The men were warned by him to stay away from Doc and Grandma's when Annie Stone, the preacher's new wife, was staying with them, and they've heeded that warning up to now. But as Mr. Van Cleet said earlier, Mr. Berg probably won't be coming into town as often – he lives out at the Triple-C Ranch with the Cooke brothers now. The men may try to sneak a peek at the girl once they figure it out."

"From the sounds of it, I don't fancy meeting the man either. I'll do my best to see she's protected." He held out his hand to August.

"See to it you do," August said as he took his hand and gave it a healthy shake.

"I thank you for hiring me on, Mr. Van Cleet. I don't know what I would have done had I not stumbled upon your town."

"Oh, somebody would've found you come spring, but you'd be a might sadder-looking than you are now!" Mr. Van Cleet said, one eyebrow arched.

August laughed, while Bowen forced a smile. They had no idea how close he'd come to becoming no more than a frozen lump in Clear Creek's main street. Now that he thought on it, it really was a miracle that he'd happened upon the tiny town. Maybe his luck was changing after all.

Several days went by, and Elsie could stand it no longer. She hadn't been out of the house since the day she'd found Bowen Drake lying frozen in the snow. Fetching wood from the small shed out back or going to the barn didn't count. She wanted to meet people, and missed spending time at the local mercantile in Nowhere. She'd loved talking with Mrs. Quinn, the owner, who kept everyone up on the latest gossip. Not that any of it was really gossip – Nowhere was so small, a person could say something at one end of town and the folks at the other end could hear it for themselves! Still, there was joy in visiting with Mrs. Quinn and the other residents.

She wondered if the Dunnigans would be as much fun. She hoped so. Mrs. Dunnigan seemed polite enough when she'd been introduced to her and her husband Wilfred the day she'd arrived. And she knew the woman was an incredible cook. But she'd overheard Grandma talk about Mrs. Dunnigan to Grandpa the night before, and apparently the woman could be a trial at times, even if she meant well.

She looked up from the book she'd been leafing through at the kitchen table. "Grandma?"

"Yes, child?"

"Would you mind very much if I went down to the Dunnigans' and looked around? I haven't visited the mercantile yet, and I wanted to see what sort of yarn and fabric they carry."

"Why, certainly. You can go anytime you want. Land sakes, it's practically right across the street!"

True, Dunnigan's Mercantile was no more than a stone's throw from the Wallers' front door – if you had a strong arm, at least. Elsie wondered why she hadn't asked before. Probably because she didn't want Grandma and Grandpa Waller fussing over her inquisitive nature – she'd had enough of that back in Nowhere. Grandpa Teddy hardly let her out of his sight when he first took charge of her after her parents died. It took a few years before he'd let her go into town on her own, or play with the other children after school in front of the mercantile before going home. Sometimes, Mrs. Quinn had been waiting on the porch steps with candy, and lucky was the child who happened to go home past the mercantile those days!

Elsie sighed. From the sounds of it, Mrs. Dunnigan would more than likely be waiting on the porch steps with a ladle in her hand waiting to smack anyone to come within range! She shuddered at the thought. "Thank you, Grandma. I'll be back as soon as I can."

Grandma Waller looked up from the vegetables she was chopping to put into a stew. "Take your time, child. In fact, I could do with a few things – let me make you a list and give you some money."

"Of course," Elsie said as she watched the woman look for something to write with.

After a few minutes, Grandma had scribbled out her list, given her some money from a crock jar on the kitchen window sill, and walked her to the door. "I gave you a little extra in case you fancy some yarn and needles. I have some, but both sets of needles are in use. I'm sure you'll be wanting to make a few things for Christmas."

"Yes, I'd like that." Grandma smiled, but Elsie could see something was wrong. "Is everything all right?"

"Of course. I was just thinking how nice it is to have you here. You can run and fetch things for me now and then, just as you're doing now. It's a great help."

Elsie stiffened at a twinge of panic. Grandpa Teddy hadn't been much older than Grandma Waller, and she knew well how a man or woman getting on in years started to slow down, how easily things could go wrong with their health, their hearts. Just as it had with Teddy …

She swallowed back her fear and smiled. Grandma Waller was too feisty to have anything happen to her for a good long while. She turned to take her coat off the rack near the door, her eyes stinging with unshed tears.

Grandma will *live a good long while! Please Lord, I can't lose her like I lost Grandpa Teddy!* Forcing her voice to not quaver, she said, "I'll be back soon."

"Take your time, child. There's no rush."

Elsie put on her coat, dropped the money Grandma gave her into her pocket, and left the house. The wind bit into her as soon as she stepped off the porch. It was like walking through ice. But she'd been through worse in Nowhere. She trod on, wondering what talk there might be in the mercantile concerning it.

The east wind whipped between the buildings, lifted her coattails into the air, and pulled her hair from its pins. It seemed as if it took forever to go the short distance to the mercantile, and by the time Elsie got through the door, her cheeks burned from the cold.

All heads turned as she entered. Apparently, everyone else had had the same idea and decided to venture out to see what was happening with the weather. The place was packed with townsfolk. Correction: men. *Lots* of men.

She stopped short as she took in the faces staring at her. Handsome ones, though. She rather thought she'd died and gone to Heaven. But her smile faded when she noticed their expressions. They weren't friendly – in fact, they looked downright mean …

"What's everybody looking at?" she demanded. Diplomacy was not one of Elsie's strong points.

Two men in the back laughed. "Isn't it obvious?" one of them said. "You, of course!"

Elsie glanced around and realized that she was the only female in the mercantile. She swallowed hard. Several of them smiled at her as they formed a half-circle around her, then turned toward the others. Were they protecting her? Or claiming her first?

The two who'd laughed when she entered tried to

shove their way past the wall surrounding her. "Stand aside and let's have a look!"

"No." said one, a tall fellow with raven-black hair. He looked to be only a few years older than she was.

"Stand aside, Ryder. She's not your type."

"Nor is she yours," Ryder said. "Besides, Mr. Van Cleet gave us orders …"

"To perdition with his orders! You know how long it's been since I seen a woman younger'n my ma?" the man whined

"I don't know and I don't care, Brett. What the man says goes."

The bell over the door tinkled, and all eyes turned toward the sound. Elsie could feel a familiar presence behind her. She spun around, hoping she knew whose eyes she'd meet.

Bowen Drake it was. The sight of him took her breath away, literally. She gasped, took a step back … and tripped.

The man called Ryder grabbed her and helped her back onto her feet from behind, as Bowen Drake grabbed one of her hands and pulled her forward. But between Ryder's pushing and Bowen's pulling there was too much momentum. She fell forward and smacked her face against Bowen's hard chest.

"Oops." Ryder commented dryly. "Sorry about that, ma'am. And about Brett back there."

"Hey!" Brett objected.

Elsie could feel the glare Bowen was giving Brett even before she looked up at his face. "I'm … I'm sorry. I seem to have lost my balance."

He looked down at her, his face stern. "That's not all you've lost." He held up several hairpins.

"Oh, dear," she said softly, taking them from him.

"Thank you. The wind is … er, quite strong today."

He did his best not to laugh, and kept it down to one snort. About half the other men in the room showed no such restraint, but stopped when he spoke. "Enough! You men have dallied here too long already! Time to get back to work!" he barked.

Some of the men grumbled, but suddenly snapped to attention when Mrs. Dunnigan popped out from a curtained doorway to one side of the counter. "Who wanted the peppermint sticks?" she yelled.

Several men raised their hands.

"Get your candy, men, then get back to the hotel! The place won't build itself!" Bowen shouted.

Elsie watched, amazed, as the men gathered around Mrs. Dunnigan. Mr. Dunnigan then appeared with several jars in his hands. "What's going on?"

Now Bowen Drake laughed. It was a wonderful sound and Elsie wanted to hear him do it again. "It's payday for the men, and Mr. Van Cleet told me that Mrs. Dunnigan has been rationing the candy of late. She's been hiding it upstairs because she's afraid it won't last until she can get more in. The men do love their sweets."

Elsie watched as men vied for position at the counter to choose what they wanted. She turned to Bowen. "Is Clear Creek that cut off then? Will no supplies really be brought in until spring?"

"Mr. Bennett says some will get through, but nothing like when the weather is good. Mr. Dunnigan told me yesterday it's going to be a hard winter, judging from the weather we're having now."

"I suppose this means you'll be wintering here then?" She tried to keep the hopeful sound in her voice to a

minimum. She hadn't seen Mr. Van Cleet's workers all

in one place until now, but though there were more than a few handsome gentlemen among them, she still favored Bowen. Her back was all a tingle just standing near him. Perhaps too near him. She took a few steps to the side for propriety's sake.

"Indeed. I don't relish freezing half to death again, Miss, um …"

"Waller. Elsie Waller," she said with a little curtsy.

"… Miss Waller. I remembered only your first name from the other day. I, ah … I do thank you again for finding me."

"Someone would have eventually found you, Mr. Drake. I just happened to be the one in a hurry to get home, so I found you first."

"*Eventually* could have been too late for me, Miss Waller. Who knows how long it would have been before someone else came along?"

She smiled. "The important thing is that you're well, Mr. Drake. I hope you've suffered no ill effects."

He looked down at her and stared at her face a moment before he spoke. "No."

A chill went up her spine and she could feel her arms break out in gooseflesh. She was glad for the coat that covered her. "I'm happy to hear it. Now, I'd better get what I came for–"

"I think it might be best if you waited a moment, Miss Waller. The men will start clearing out soon."

She looked up at him. "What about you? Are you here to buy some candy, too?"

He stared at her face briefly. "Something sweet … does sound nice. May I buy you a lemon drop, Miss Waller?"

Elsie suddenly couldn't talk. Another shiver went up

her spine and she had to fight to keep her body from

trembling. "Why … thank you, Mr. Drake. That would be lovely."

Five

BOWEN TURNED AS A BLAST of wind entered the mercantile. "Howdy, Preacher!" a man yelled over the throng.

"Hello, there!" the newcomer called back. "Good heavens, what's everybody doing here?"

"Payday! It's our break, and we come to get a few things before the mercantile closes," a man nearby explained.

"I see," the preacher said. "Well then, you can all take a gander at this when you're done making your purchases." He turned and made his way to a small table and two chairs set up near one of the front windows. "Wilfred?" he called over his shoulder.

"Right here, Preacher Jo! Whatcha be needin'?" Wilfred Dunnigan called from behind the store counter.

"May I pin this notice up here? Or is there a better place?"

"What notice?"

"It's to announce the Christmas play!"

Everyone went silent. Bowen and Elsie glanced at the many faces of the men in the mercantile, all of which had turned toward the preacher.

"Christmas play?" one of them whispered in awe.

"Does this mean you'll be needin' people to act out parts and suchlike?" another asked suspiciously.

"Why, yes," the preacher replied. "As a matter of fact, it does."

"I ain't gonna get up on no stage!" one yelled in terror.

"Me neither! And you can't make me!" called out another.

"No one's making anyone," the preacher assured them with a chuckle. "But anyone who wants to can try out."

"Well, I want to," one man said calmly. "I'd love to be in a play."

"Put it up on that there board next to the door, Preacher Jo," Wilfred said. "If you put it over the table, folks'll be hanging over my head to look at it while I'm playing checkers. Might disturb my moves and cost me a game."

The preacher smiled at the crowd, then turned and walked to a wide board nailed into the wall next to the door. It already had a few notices pinned to it. Bowen hadn't noticed it when he came in, probably because all he'd noticed was the beautiful girl who now stood at his side.

When the preacher was done, he walked over to Bowen. "Hello, young man. I don't believe we've met."

"Bowen Drake, Reverend. I'm …" He sighed. "I'm new here."

"Mr. Drake is working for Mr. Van Cleet," Miss Waller volunteered.

The preacher looked from one face to the other. "Ahhhh, you must be the man Miss Waller rescued."

Miss Waller looked away, her face red. Bowen felt himself pinking up as well. Is that what the talk around town was, that he'd been rescued by a woman? Oh, good grief! He was glad that the last gang he rode with wasn't there to hear this! But then, it was true – hadn't he thanked her for doing just that?

He sighed again, this time in resignation. "Yes, Miss Waller came along just in the nick of time." He looked at her, but she still had her face turned away. No matter – from what he could see through her wild, windswept hair, her red-tipped ears told him she was still blushing. Or maybe she was still cold – she'd left her house with only her coat and no bonnet, which explained the hair-pins he'd found on the mercantile steps. What was she thinking, coming out in this wind without proper attire?

"Are you going to try out for a part, Mr. Drake? We'd love to have you get to know our little community, and a play is a great way to do it." The preacher stood and stared at him before he smiled and turned to Miss Waller. "And, what about you? We're going to need someone to play Mary."

"M–Mary?" Miss Waller said, her eyes wide. "Are you doing the Christmas story?"

The preacher gave them a tight-lipped smile. "Yes, we are."

"Oh, I love the Christmas story! Do you really think I'd make a good Mary?"

"My wife and I will be assigning parts this week. Come to the church tomorrow and we'll let you have a go at it." He again looked at Bowen who, if he could have, would have slunk behind Miss Waller and blended in with the bolts of fabric stacked on a nearby table. But no, the preacher looked him right in the eye. "You might make a good Joseph, Mr. Drake. Have you ever acted in a play before?"

It was all Bowen could do to keep from laughing. What else had he been doing for the last three years? He'd been playing the part of an outlaw for longer than he'd care to admit. And wasn't that all it was, an act? How long was this show he'd placed himself in going to run? How long before he tired of it? After all, it hadn't done him much good – his heart was no better off. Nor had it shamed his father into sobering up, or caused his professors to stop bragging about him. And for crying out loud, in all that time he hadn't even been able to pull off anything illegal! He wasn't even good at the role!

He finally shook himself out of his reverie and told the preacher, "it's been a long time since I've been in a play." He'd actually been in a couple of amateur productions while at Harvard, but he sure didn't want to bring that up here.

"Well, an educated man like you should have no problem with one of the bigger parts. I hear tell you can read and write."

Bowen raised a curious brow. "How did you know that?"

The preacher laughed. "Mr. Drake, you'd be quick to learn that in a town this size, news travels fast. Why don't you come to the church tomorrow after work with Miss Waller and take a look at our script? I'm sure you could memorize the lines with no problem."

Bowen's jaw dropped. Why was he letting himself get roped into this? *Tell the man no!*

But he didn't get the chance. "Oh, that sounds fine!" Miss Waller exclaimed with a little clap of her hands.

"It, it does?" Bowen blurted back.

"Of course it does!" added the preacher. "I'll see the two of you tomorrow. In fact, why don't you join me and the wife for supper down at the saloon after we go over the parts?"

Bowen was frozen in confusion. What kind of a town was this? The preacher and his wife ate dinner in the saloon? The men were spending their payday money on candy before whiskey? Come to think of it, he'd never seen any of the men return from the saloon drunk – happy and laughing, maybe, but never senseless. Maybe Mr. Van Cleet didn't want them drinking too much, and they behaved themselves to keep their jobs.

He hadn't been to the saloon since the day he thawed out. There was a woman named Sally Upton who cooked at the hotel. He'd helped August and some of the other men set up the new cookstove and put up shelves in the hotel kitchen on his first day of work. She put it to use right away, making meals for the hotel staff (and Bowen) while the bulk of the men spent their lunch breaks (and in most cases, their evenings) at the saloon. Not getting drunk …

"Mr. Drake?"

Bowen blinked twice and returned his attention to Miss Waller. "Oh, uh, yes. That would be … nice."

"Miss Waller? You'll be able to join us, won't you?" the preacher asked.

"Of course! I wouldn't miss it – I love plays!"

The excited look on her beautiful face made Bowen smile. "You're not afraid to be in front of a crowd, Miss Waller?"

"Oh no, not me! I used to tell the younger children stories after school in front of the mercantile when Mrs. Quinn – she's the store owner – would let me. I'd act out most of the parts. When I was through, Mrs. Quinn would sometimes give all of us a piece of candy."

He smiled down at her. "I see. And you'd find playing Mary exciting?"

"Oh, of course!"

"I'll play Joseph if'n Mr. Drake don't want to!" a man with missing teeth spoke loudly.

"Me, too!" called another as the men, small white candy sacks in hand, began to encircle them again.

"Preacher Jo!" yet another man said. "Not all of us can have the part, and Mr. Drake don't seem to want it. Why don't the rest of us draw straws?"

Bowen recognized the lustful gleam in the eyes of a

few, while others only wanted an excuse to be near the lovely Miss Waller. He needed to act quickly. "We'll see you tomorrow to discuss the play and join you for supper, Reverend," he said as he eyed the men. They began to back up, some grumbling as they did.

"Well if'n I cain't play Joseph, then don't expect me to play some critter!" the man with the missing teeth huffed. "I'll be one of them wise men!"

"That'd be a first for you, Jake!" a man shouted from the crowd, and most of the others laughed. Jake scowled in embarrassment and left the store. The remaining men started to file out the door and head back to work as well.

The preacher chuckled as he watched them go before he turned back to Bowen. "Forgive me – with all this talk of the play, I seem to have forgotten to introduce myself. The Reverend Josiah King, at your service. Though most folks around here have taken to calling me 'Preacher Jo'."

Bowen smiled. "It seems Mr. Van Cleet's men aren't too keen on taking part in your play, Preacher Jo."

"Oh, a few will want to, I'm sure. As for the others, we do need *someone* in the audience. It's the rest of the town I'm concerned with."

Wilfred sauntered over to the doors of the mercantile and read the notice. "The Christmas story, huh? Hmmm, I think I could handle a part."

"Do you now, Wilfred? That would be great! Come to the church tomorrow with Mr. Drake and Miss Waller here." He looked past Wilfred to his wife, who was stashing candy jars under the counter. "And what about you, Mrs. Dunnigan? Would you be interested in having a part in our play?"

"Have you gone plumb loco? You're not getting me up on a stage!"

They all chuckled at that. Even Bowen had learned over the past few days that Irene Dunnigan wasn't afraid of anything. He doubted stage fright would be an issue. But she was clearly as stubborn as she was courageous, and once she had made up her mind, it would take an act of God to change it.

"Well, I'm sure we'll need someone to be in charge of refreshments. Why don't you talk to my wife about it?"

Mrs. Dunnigan's face lit up with a smile. "I'll do that." She then turned to Wilfred. "Let's get the rest of this candy back upstairs and stash it, or there won't be enough for those men when they come in next week."

Wilfred nodded and winked at them. "Duty calls. I'll see you all tomorrow." The Dunnigans scooped up the remaining jars of candy and disappeared behind the curtained doorway. Preacher Jo, with a nod and a smile, left the mercantile himself.

Bowen, realizing that he and Miss Waller were now alone, turned and stared at the wondrous creature next to him – and once again, the sight of her took his breath away. It wasn't just that she was pretty. He felt a special connection to her, a bond. How, he didn't know, but it was there. Perhaps it was because she had saved his life – he was truly grateful for that. "You'll make a fine Mary."

She looked at him and smiled. "You'll do well as Joseph, I'm sure. I suppose this means we'll be spending a lot of time together… since we'll have to practice and all."

Bowen hadn't thought of that, but she was right. If they were playing the main parts they'd need the most practice, wouldn't they? Maybe being in this play wasn't so bad after all …

"I wonder what other parts there are," she said, pulling him from his thoughts.

Bowen looked into her eyes and had the sudden urge to kiss her. It shocked him, and he took a step back to put some distance between them. He hadn't thought much about women in some time, not after those years when any woman he was with wound up with someone else. So, why bother? But this one ... he lifted his hat off his head and ran a hand through his hair. "I guess we'll find out tomorrow."

"Well ... I suppose I should get what I came for." She looked around nervously as she pulled a list out of her reticule. "I wonder when the Dunnigans will come back. Mrs. Dunnigan will have to fetch some of this for me, I'm sure."

"They should be back downstairs soon. Is there anything ... *I* can do for you?" Not that he could do much, except maybe get something off a high shelf for her. But he wasn't ready to leave her yet, and didn't want her to be alone. No telling if one of the men might come back – and she really shouldn't be unescorted ...

She smiled up at him. "Why, that's so kind of you to offer, Mr. Drake."

Bowen smiled back, and hoped her list was a long one.

Six

THE NEXT MORNING, ELSIE FOUND herself once again at the mercantile. The ladies' sewing circle had decided to meet in town, as it was easier and closer for most of the ladies to get to. They usually met out at the Triple-C Ranch, but with the current weather it was too far to go for some.

Elsie tensely watched as Harrison Cooke's wife Sadie put a hand to her mouth and pressed her lips together.

"Again?" Grandma said exasperated. "Land sakes, child! Why did you even come?"

Sadie quickly got up and made for the curtained doorway behind the store counter. Grandma and Mrs. Mulligan shook their heads.

"I'm glad I didn't get so sick when I was expecting little Liam," Lucy White said softly.

"She does have it bad," Mrs. Mulligan agreed.

"Well, if you ask me, she should keep a peppermint in her mouth at all times!" Mrs. Dunnigan huffed.

"The peppermint doesn't help anymore, Auntie." Belle Cooke told her. "She tried."

Elsie smiled as she worked on her stitching. Belle Cooke was married to Colin, the happy-go-lucky middle brother. She was also Mr. and Mrs. Dunnigan's niece, which surprised Elsie at first. Belle had been a Boston socialite before coming to Clear Creek. Seemed the little town was full of surprises.

Speaking of which, Cozette Cooke, the new Duchess

of Stantham, was also present. She was married to the eldest brother, Duncan, the one who'd inherited a title and estate in England. The enchanting fairy-like woman with the tanned face looked less like a duchess than like the frontier girl she'd grown up as, but there it was.

And next to Cozette were a tall elegant woman and her equally regal daughter. They had been introduced as Mrs. Duprie and Mrs. Berg, but Grandma had reminded Elsie over breakfast that they were in fact a countess and a princess. And the countess was the duchess's new step-mother, which made the duchess and the princess ... it was a lot to take in. She was starting to think she should draw a diagram, just to keep them all straight.

Needless to say, there hadn't been any sort of royalty back in Nowhere – though if Nellie Davis had her way, she'd have crowned herself queen! Elsie hid a smile. Nellie was as far from being a queen as Elsie was; she just enjoyed acting like one ...

"Have you read the notice about the play?" Mabel Turner asked.

Elsie stopped her stitching. "I was there when the preacher came in to post it. He invited me to the church this afternoon to try out for a part."

"I might join you," Belle Cooke said. "I think a play is a lovely idea. I'm not sure I want a part, but I could help make the costumes if needed."

"I'm sure Preacher Jo would appreciate any help you ladies offered up," Grandma said.

Sadie quietly returned and took her seat. Her face was pale and she looked like she needed to lie down. Grandma took one look at her and shook her head.

"I'll be fine," Sadie insisted. "It can't last much longer, after all."

"When I was carrying Tommy, mine lasted for months

and months," Mabel said. "Not so bad as you, but bad enough."

Sadie groaned.

"How is ... Tommy?" Cozette asked. Elsie noticed the woman's odd speech. Grandma had told her that Cozette had been mute for a number of years, and had only recently learned to speak again.

"Doc's out with him now," Mabel said. "That's how I was able to come join y'all today. He's checking on Tommy, then was going to go out to ... where did he say?"

"The Triple-C, to check on one of the hands," Grandma finished for her. "Got gouged by a bull – ain't that right, Sadie?"

"Yes, that's ... oh dear ..." Sadie again threw a hand over her mouth.

"I hear that if you take deep breaths it helps," Elsie quickly offered.

Sadie tried it and took one deep breath, two, three ... "Oh dear!" She once again jumped up and ran for the back of the mercantile.

"That poor girl might as well carry her own bucket with her," Mrs. Dunnigan said, shaking her head in either annoyance or sympathy. With Mrs. Dunnigan, it was hard to tell sometimes.

The women smiled at the remark when suddenly the mercantile door flew open and one of Mr. Van Cleet's men stumbled in. "Grandma Waller! Where's Doc?"

"Out at the Turner farm. What's all the ruckus?"

"There's been an accident! Bill Smith is hurt pretty bad!"

Grandma immediately set down her sewing and stiffly stood. "Take me to him. Elsie, run to the house and get Doc's spare bag. It's in the kitchen in the sideboard cupboard."

"Yes, ma'am!" Elsie set her sewing aside and also stood. Both women went to the coat rack near the mercantile's front doors and grabbed their shawls. They wrapped themselves up and left, Grandma for the hotel, Elsie for the house.

Elsie ran into the house, found the bag, then hurried back down the street. She hadn't been to the hotel as yet, and wasn't sure what to expect when she got there. The injured man must be inside, since that was where all the work was taking place. Sure enough, when she went through the main double doors of the building, she immediately noticed a crowd of men near the staircase. But where was Grandma?

"I don't believe it! Where'd you learn how to do that, son? And so fast!"

Elsie followed the sound of Grandma's voice and pushed between the onlookers to get to the woman. She found her crouched next to a man on the floor along with Bowen Drake. The injured man had a broken leg that had already been splinted.

Bowen shrugged. "I … learned a few things along the trail out west."

"That's the fastest I've ever heard of someone splinting a leg, even faster than Doc. What did you come fetch me for?"

"He weren't fixed when I come to get ya," the man who'd fetched her from the mercantile said. "But he was moanin' and carryin' on somethin' awful!"

"If you have any laudanum to give him, it would help." Bowen told her.

"I got some. Elsie?"

" Here I am," Elsie said, handing her the bag. She stared at Bowen Drake bent over Bill Smith, deftly checking him for other injuries. If this is what Mr. Drake had learned along the trail, he'd learned it very well.

Grandma took a small bottle from the bag. "Do you know how much to give him?"

Bowen looked hesitant at first, then finally said. "I do."

Grandma eyed him suspiciously for a moment before she handed him the bottle. "Somebody get a glass of water." One of the men in the crowd disappeared.

While he was gone, Bowen had several others help him get Bill onto a cot. By the time the man returned with the water, they had him settled. Bowen took the water from him and Elsie watched as he put a measured amount of laudanum into the glass then stirred it with his finger. "Here, Bill, drink this. It'll help with the pain."

Bill took the mixture gratefully, drank it, made a face, then handed the glass back to Bowen.

"You men carry this cot back to your quarters," he said, then looked at the patient. "I'll see to it your dinner is brought to you."

"Much obliged, Mr. Drake. And thank ya! My leg's sure to heal nice and straight the way you done fixed it!"

"Let's hope so," Bowen said as he patted him on the shoulder. "Get some rest, Bill. I'm sure Doc Waller will want to check on you as soon as he gets back to town."

Elsie noticed that Grandma had gone silent. She was watching Bowen carefully, but offered no assistance.

"I'm sure he will. Glad you were here to help, though," Bill said with a rasp, as several others lifted the cot to take him back to the main sleeping quarters.

Once they were gone, Bowen then turned to those remaining. "Okay, back to work. Mr. Bennett is expecting those three upper rooms to be walled this afternoon. And for crying out loud, watch where you step." The men dispersed and returned to work, and he gave his attention to Grandma and Elsie. "Thank you for the use of the laudanum," he said as he handed the bottle back to Grandma.

"You'd best keep it for now – he'll probably do with another dose come morning," she told him. "I must say, for a man who picked up a little doctoring know-how along the trail, you must've got a double dose. That leg was set mighty fine, son."

Bowen gave her the barest of smiles. "I did what anyone else would have done."

"Anyone else wouldn't have set it the way you did," Grandma replied. "They wouldn't have known how."

Bowen shrugged, then tipped his hat. "If you'll excuse me, ladies, I'd best get back to work myself."

"Yes, I suppose you should," Grandma said quietly. She took Elsie by the arm and started to steer her toward the door. "And we'd best get back to the mercantile. Poor Mrs. Turner and Fannie Fig will be dying to know what happened."

"Who's Fannie Fig, Grandma? I didn't meet anyone by that name this morning." Elsie said.

"That's because she's usually late unless she rides with someone else. She's bound to be there by now."

Elsie turned to get one last glimpse at Bowen Drake and unexpectedly met with his warm brown eyes. She felt a blush creep into her cheeks as he offered her a smile and watched her go.

"There's more to that boy than meets the eye." Grandma said softly as they left through the hotel's double doors and went out to the street.

Elsie pondered her words as they headed back to the mercantile. Here she'd been wondering how to make sure Mr. Drake discovered how interesting she could be, and now he held her interest!

What more could she learn about the mysterious Mr. Drake? Perhaps that afternoon at the church she'd find out …

"'Thuh-reee', oh, that ain't right. Ahhhh … 'Th-there wha … wha … whaz no roooom … at the inn'," Willie the stagecoach driver read. He looked up from the script in his hand and gave Preacher Jo and his wife Annie a wide grin. His two front teeth were missing. "How was that?" he asked proudly. "I do all right?"

Preacher Jo smiled at the look of triumph on Willie's face. "That was fine, Willie. We have lots of things that need to be done. What would you like to do to help? Play a part or help build the manger? I know what I think you should do because I know you'd be great at it, but what do you think?"

Willie scratched his head. "Well, I know I don't read so good, but I am pretty good with mah hands …"

"Which would you prefer?" Annie asked with a smile.

"Aw shucks, Mrs. Preacher, I'd be more comfortable buildin' the manger. What if I cain't 'member mah lines when it's time?"

"You would do well at either task, Willie. But it's the one you feel most comfortable with that you should pick," she told him warmly.

"I'll build the manger, then. I'd be real good at that. 'Sides, I've got time right now."

Which was very true. The stage couldn't run in weather like this. Willie, like everyone else in Clear Creek, would have to stay put for the winter.

"Then what say we put you in charge of the manger?" Preacher Jo told him. "In fact, why don't you pick out a couple of men to help you? We'll need a stable as well."

"Me?" Willie asked, surprised. "In charge? I ain't never been put in charge of nothin' – 'cept drivin' the stage, of course, but I don't think that counts."

"Of course it does," Annie told him. "Who do you want to help you?"

Willie studied the dozen or so men who'd showed up to take part in the play. "Gosh, Mrs. King, I dunno. Which one o' you fellers wants to help me?" Six hands shot up, and Willie took a step back. "Um … I think we're gonna have to draw straws or somethin', Mrs. King. I dunno who to pick."

Preacher Jo laughed. "You do whatever you need to help you choose. In the meantime, which of you gentlemen would like to read for the part of the narrator?"

Harvey Brown, a local farmer, raised his hand.

"Ah, Harvey – so glad to see you volunteer. Come up here and have a go at it, then."

Bowen leaned over to Elsie. "Is it just me, or have you noticed how the preacher and his wife are giving everyone a chance to read, even though they already know some of them can't?"

"Yes, I noticed."

Bowen smiled. The thought warmed him. Everyone would have their chance at a part, then get to pick what they wanted to do based on their own strengths. Very clever. No wonder the men who'd tried out so far were full of smiles. They were given a chance to do what they knew they were good at, as well as a chance to step out of their comfort zone and try something new.

And it worked – one of them had gotten the part of the innkeeper, even though he couldn't read a whit. Another had gotten the part of his wife! With so few women in town, that was inevitable … but then, hadn't all the women's parts in Shakespeare's day been played by men? Bowen tried to imagine one of the rough-hewn Westerners in the pews playing Portia or Beatrice, and had to suppress a chuckle.

"I'm glad we get to go last," Elsie said. "I wouldn't want our ability to read to discourage anyone."

"I don't think anything would discourage this bunch, Miss Waller. Preacher Jo knows exactly what he's doing. He truly cares for the people in this town."

Elsie smiled. "Yes, he does." She readjusted herself in the pew. They were sitting near the back of the church with a few others as they waited their turn. They'd been there an hour already. She'd been under the impression that only she and Bowen would be at the church that afternoon, but half the town had showed up! There would be no time for dinner with Preacher Jo and his wife at this rate.

"Am I late?" a shrill voice asked behind them.

Harvey Brown stopped reading and looked up as everyone turned around.

Fannie Fig made her way into the pew behind Bowen and Elsie, and sat beside Mrs. Mulligan. Everything was silent for a moment before Harvey started reading again, his voice clear and precise.

"Not really," Mrs. Mulligan whispered. "Preacher Jo hasn't got to the costume-making yet. That's what I'm here for."

"Oh, not me – I want to play a part! Did I ever tell you I played Juliet once? Well, I did, and I was quite good if I do say so myself."

"Then you'd best sit up front with the others," Elsie told her in a low voice. "They're reading for the part of the narrator right now."

Suddenly everyone clapped and Elsie and the others

gave their attention to the front.

"A fine job, Harvey!" Preacher Jo said. "Would you like to be the narrator or do something else?"

"Oh, I'd like to be the narrator!"

"Then the part is yours."

The men sitting up front all sighed in relief. Some went so far as to wipe their brows with a handkerchief. Preacher Jo chuckled at that before he called out, "Mary?"

Elsie started, then realized the Rev. King was addressing Mrs. Mulligan.

Mrs. Mulligan stood. "Yes, Preacher Jo?"

"I'll send you those who've been assigned their parts. I leave their costuming in your capable hands."

Mrs. Mulligan beamed as Harvey Brown and several other men headed to the back of the church. "I'll fix them right up, Preacher Jo!"

"Better put the word out, Mary, and get yourself some help. It's too big a task for one woman to take on," he told her.

"Oh, don't you worry – Sadie and Belle Cooke will help me," she said happily as she eyed the short, rotund form of Harvey Brown approaching.

"Maybe we should go sit up front," Bowen suggested.

"I think perhaps you're right," Elsie agreed.

She was shocked when he took her hand in his and pulled her to her feet. Her eyes grew round as saucers as he led her from the pew and out to the aisle. His hand was big, warm, and the roughness of it sent a thrill of excitement through her.

He must have realized what he'd done, because he suddenly dropped her hand like a hot potato.

Disappointment sank into Elsie's heart. What was he doing? If he didn't want to hold her hand, why take it in the first place? She fought against a sigh as she followed him up the aisle and took a seat in the second pew from the front. Preacher Jo smiled at her as she sat, then gave Bowen a small nod. They were going to read next.

The men who were left at the front of the church were assigned their parts, Wilfred Dunnigan among them. They went to the rear of the church, where Mary Mulligan already had her tape measure out. Wilfred winked at Elsie as he passed. "I'm a wise man," he said proudly and patted his chest.

"Looks like we're next," Bowen said in a low voice. Elsie briefly wondered if he was going to take her hand again. But instead, he stood, and without another word went to the front of the church.

His attention elsewhere, Elsie let go the sigh she'd been holding back. It looked like the only hand-holding she was going to get was if she held her own. Bowen was suddenly acting like he wanted to be as far from her as he could get. She'd never seen anyone leave a pew so fast.

Well, whatever had prompted him to take her hand earlier wasn't there now. But didn't Joseph have to hold Mary's hand somewhere in the play? Surely she could improvise something – and if it were part of the play no one would think it improper.

She watched and listened as Bowen read, quite expertly, some of Joseph's lines. His voice carried well, and he made good use of facial expressions. He looked right at her when he finished and smiled.

Oh, why did he have to have such a wonderful smile? What was she to do? He was so handsome, and he'd need to spend a lot of time with her if they were to be ready on Christmas Eve. Beyond that, who knew? And then spring would come and Bowen Drake, in all likelihood, would be gone.

Elsie stared at her folded hands in her lap. If she wasn't careful, she'd be left behind with a broken heart. What had she been thinking, trying to get the man to notice her? Was she being foolish? Or was she, as usual, just trying to take on another adventure?

But she knew she had to be careful – this adventure could cost her, her heart.

Seven

THE TOWN WAS ABUZZ THE next several days with talk of the play. Some boasted about having a speaking part, others preened over the wonderful costumes. Some were as nervous as a cat on a string swinging over a pack of hungry dogs (Wilfred Dunnigan's description), others were as cool as the weather outside.

Elsie was one of the latter – and that was the problem. She had no trouble memorizing her lines. But how was she going to spend more time with Bowen Drake if she didn't need to rehearse? Well, perhaps *he* did. She hadn't seen him much since they'd read together for Preacher Jo on Thursday. Tomorrow was Sunday, and everyone was to meet at the church after lunch to begin practice. If she was lucky, he hadn't had time to practice because he was too busy working.

She threw caution to the wind for a moment and let her heart fly where it would, only to reel it in and lock it up the next. She always had been a free spirit and a bit headstrong, and was well known back in Nowhere to leap before she looked. Grandpa Teddy was forever telling her that might get her into trouble one day. So here she was, trying to heed his wise words (which usually amounted to "Good God, Elsie! What were you thinking?") and decide on the best course of action regarding Bowen Drake. But no matter how much her head cautioned her heart, her heart wouldn't listen and went its own way.

"Oh Grandpa Teddy, I just don't know what to do!" she said to herself as she paced around her small room. She felt silly talking to someone who wasn't there, and dead besides, but she'd often done the same thing as a child with her deceased mother. No one ever talked back – if they had, it would've scared the wadding out of her! – but it seemed to help.

She supposed she should be talking to the Almighty about it, but what if *He* said forget it, move on, find another man to dream about? No, no – once she set her sights on something, she went after it wholeheartedly.

Of course, until this point, it hadn't involved the possibility of a broken heart …

Elsie had suffered a broken heart before – losing her parents as a child, and more recently when she lost Grandpa Teddy. But this was different – a failed romance could conceivably kill you. At least according to Mrs. Quinn, who used to tell her stories of young lovers, their heartbreaks and, in some cases, subsequent deaths.

She shuddered at the thought, and grabbed her shawl that she'd thrown over a chair earlier. Maybe if she went down to the mercantile, it would clear her head. In fact, she had some pennies set aside – perhaps a few pieces of candy might settle her nerves!

She ran down the stairs and headed for the door.

"Where in blazes are you going in such a hurry?" Grandpa Waller called from the dining parlor. He was sitting at the table, writing in a notebook.

Elsie stopped up short. "Just to the mercantile, Grandpa – I've a hankering for something sweet."

"Your Grandma just baked some cookies."

"I know, but …"

"Well, I understand it's hard to be cooped up in a house all day when you're a young 'un. Go on then, have a visit with Mrs. Dunnigan. But bring me back some peppermints!"

Elsie smiled as she went out the door and shut it behind her. The mercantile was a hub of activity these days. The old one had burned down in the summer, but a new one had been built quicker than a wink. Grandpa told her the new one was much bigger and better than the old. It was bright and cheery, with large windows in front and a high ceiling. Folks sometimes came there just to visit each other, and it had become the logical winter meeting place for the ladies' sewing circle.

And Mrs. Dunnigan couldn't be happier – not that "happy" was exactly a normal state for her. But she'd sold more goods in the one month the new place had been open than she had in the six months prior to the old one burning down.

The bell above the door tinkled as Elsie entered. The Dunnigans had hung pine wreaths with pretty red ribbons on the doors. She loved their scent.

Fannie Fig was at the counter, speaking with Mrs. Dunnigan. Both women looked up at her, and Fanny suddenly lowered her voice conspiratorially. She whispered to Mrs. Dunnigan, stole a glance in Elsie's direction, then shook her head with a tsk-tsk-tsk sound.

Elsie blushed red. Was she telling Mrs. Dunnigan about Bowen's impromptu hand- holding from the other day? But what of it? They were simply leaving the pew. Why were there always folks in town, *any* town, who liked to gossip?

Fannie Fig gave Mrs. Dunnigan a curt nod, stuffed a small white sack into her reticule, picked up her packages and strode past Elsie with her head held high and nose in the air.

Elsie fought the urge to roll her eyes. The hand-holding incident was probably the talk of the town now. She braced herself as she approached the counter. "Hello, Mrs. Dunnigan!"

Mrs. Dunnigan narrowed her eyes at her and scrunched up her face. "You haven't been doin' anything improper-like, have you?"

"I beg your pardon!" Elsie asked indignantly. She'd heard Mrs. Dunnigan could be straightforward, but really!

"That Drake fella is a stranger here, girl. You'd do best to keep your distance with him until you get to know him proper."

Elsie sighed in exasperation. "How am I supposed to keep my distance *and* get to know him proper?"

Mrs. Dunnigan snorted. "I saw the way he looked at you a few days ago. He's got his mind on more than his work at the hotel. You just be sure to mind yourself!"

Elsie crossed her arms over her chest. "Mrs. Dunnigan, I don't see how it's any business of yours—"

"I watch out for the folks in this town, missy. Folks like your Grandma and Grandpa Waller. That makes it my business! And seeing as how you're their kin, that means I'm gonna watch out for you, too!"

Elsie swore the woman's words came out more like a bark. If Mrs. Dunnigan had been a dog, Elsie would be terrified. As it was, she was just angry. "Mrs. Dunnigan, I don't know what Mrs. Fig told you but …"

"Fannie Fig blows everything up bigger than it is. She told me you almost kissed the man right there in the middle of the church!"

Elsie gasped.

"Of course, I didn't believe her. But you mind yourself, missy. That Drake fella still needs to prove himself before I'll trust him! Now, what do ya want?"

A different mercantile to shop at, was the first thing that came to Elsie's mind. But instead, she handed Mrs. Dunnigan the pennies. "Peppermint candy, please."

Bowen had finished counting all the containers of nails, boards and brackets, and double-checked the tool list. Everything was accounted for. Now that he had the time, he should mosey on over to the bank and "help" put the new safe in. Not that it would be all that hard to do – it mostly would involve watching Mr. Van Cleet show off the safe's latest features.

But you really ought to practice for the play …

Now where did that thought come from? Practice for a Christmas pageant over studying the workings of a safe, one he planned on breaking into as soon as…

"What am I thinking?" he said aloud as he sat down on a nearby crate and stared at the boxes of hammers and nails. He looked around the storage room. It was tucked into a corner of the hotel, one of several, and he'd taken to using this particular one as an office of sorts.

What *was* he thinking? He had a job. He'd gone as far west as he could without drowning in the Pacific to get away from his father and from Harvard. He'd begun to make new friends, and was gaining the respect of the men he worked with. He was even being driven to distraction by a bright-eyed beauty who had *saved his life*. And he was still obsessing over a potential spot of outlawry that, knowing his luck, would end up becoming an act of charity or some such. Good grief! Why *wouldn't* he be thinking about the play?

And practice was in less than two hours. He and Miss Waller could sit in a corner of the church, going over their lines while Preacher Jo and his wife worked with the three wise men: Wilfred Dunnigan, Sheriff Hughes, and Patrick Mulligan. That would take time – and meanwhile he'd be in close proximity to Miss Elsie Waller.

Bowen closed his eyes and immediately saw her wide smile and honey-gold hair. She was a rare gem – not just because she was the prettiest girl he'd ever seen, but because she possessed a spark, a bright light that would not be put out. It was in the way she walked, the way she carried herself and held her head. She was not some demure little thing afraid of her own shadow. No, Elsie Waller had an adventurous spirit. He could tell by the way she looked people in the eye, him included. She wasn't the kind to back down, and he guessed that when she set her mind to something, she went after it with gusto.

He smiled. Was *she* the reason he'd decided to stay? He could have pushed on after he got his strength back – it would have been difficult, but not impossible. He'd heard of other men doing it. But other men didn't have a flaxen-haired beauty staring him in the face with a look of wonder every time she saw them.

And Elsie Waller's eyes did have a way of drinking a man up like a glass of cold milk after a slice of apple pie. That one quality alone had interested him from the start – the way she'd looked at him the day she found him, the day she'd held his hands to warm them. Such a little thing, but he could see in her eyes how serious she was about it.

Bowen absently stared up at the ceiling. But if he pursued her, would she suddenly turn around and find someone else like all the others had? Should he even try? His strange luck had a way of making things work out for everyone but him. Was it only a matter of time before it kicked in and he had to watch her walk down the aisle to another man standing at the end of it waiting for her?

Egads, had he just thought about Elsie Waller and *marriage* in conjunction? Maybe he should go down and watch Cyrus Van Cleet show off his new safe after all! Maybe if he had half a brain, he'd go down to the new bank and have Cyrus lock his heart up in it.

So, again, what was he thinking? The smart thing would be to stay away from the girl. This time wasn't like the others, when he'd purposely set out to win hearts then toss them aside. No, this time he was becoming increasingly interested in pursuing and capturing this particular heart … and that could prove to be quite dangerous indeed.

He set the thought aside and stood. He really ought to do his best to avoid her, but how? He was playing Joseph! How could he avoid her when he had to spend the next several weeks practicing a play with her?

Well, he could always back out – surely Preacher Jo would understand, wouldn't he? There was only one way to find out. He'd march right over to the church and tell the preacher he couldn't do it, and that he'd just have to find someone else.

But think of what you'd be giving up …

Bowen groaned aloud. He ran a hand through his hair before he grabbed his hat, put on his coat, and left the hotel.

But the voice of reason followed him. *You could start a new life here. Nobody here knows your past, after all. You could work for Mr. Van Cleet. And if you don't want to talk with your father or communicate with Harvard, then don't. They don't need to know where you are …*

He stopped halfway between the church and the hotel. "But what if they found out?" he muttered to himself

So what if they do? Do you honestly think any of them would come all the way across the country to a village in the middle of nothing just to have a cup of coffee with you and talk about the good old days?

He nodded. "There's a point."

"A point to what?"

Bowen jumped and spun to face none other than Elsie Waller.

She stood there, glancing around for a moment before turning back to him. "Who were you talking to?"

Bowen froze. How much more ridiculous could he look? He rolled his eyes in resignation. "Myself, actually."

"Oh," she said with a dismissive wave of her hand. "I do that all the time."

"You do?"

She nodded. "It used to drive my Grandpa Teddy crazy. He always thought I was talking to him when I wasn't. His hearing wasn't too good, you see."

Bowen let out a nervous chuckle. "Poor fellow."

"Not anymore. He's dead."

"Oh! I, I'm sorry!" Bowen's face went red. But she was right – Grandpa Teddy, as she called him, certainly wasn't suffering any ills now. "It's ... not a usual habit of mine, talking to myself."

"Well, perhaps it should be. It's certainly one of mine!"

Bowen couldn't help but smile. As usual, she was bright-eyed and exuberant, with an infectious energy that reached out and touched him whether he wanted it to or not. It made him want to take her in his arms and kiss her senseless. He had to swallow and look away before he became so entranced he caused a scandal.

"Are you ready for practice?" she asked.

He nodded.

"I'm looking forward to it, aren't you? This is going to be a lot of fun! Mrs. Mulligan already made the costumes for the three wise men!"

"Good, good," Bowen mumbled. She was wearing a bonnet this afternoon, and he was glad she'd be warmer. Her coat was a soft blue and of good quality. Her dress, from what he could see of it, was almost the same color as her coat, a shade darker perhaps, and set off the color of her eyes.

Think of it, Bowen ... if you stayed, she could be yours ...

He closed his eyes against the voice of reason. He knew it was only a matter of time before his luck would revert, and she would belong to someone else.

"Shall we?" she asked.

He automatically offered her his arm, and she just as automatically took it. "Is something wrong?" she asked.

Bowen sighed. It seemed that no matter what he thought about leaving town or avoiding the woman on his arm – or burgling the bank – the opposite seemed to happen. Perhaps his odd luck was changing. But if that were so, what else might happen to him while he was in Clear Creek? More importantly, what would happen to the people in it?

Eight

"THAT NIGHT, THERE WERE A few … ranchers nearby guarding their … *cows*?" Harvey Brown looked up from the piece of paper in his hand. He looked at the line again. "Ain't it supposed to be sheep?"

"I thought I'd change it up a bit, make it more relevant to today," the Rev. King explained.

Harvey's mouth twisted in confusion as he read the line to himself a few times. He then shrugged his shoulders and continued. "Suddenly out of nowhere, an angel of the Lord appeared! He was big and bright and, with one flap of his wings … blew out their *campfire*?"

Annie King put a hand to her mouth in chagrin before she turned to her husband. "Josiah King, what have you done?"

"I made it my own. What do they call it? Poetic license?"

"It's the Christmas story!"

"It's still the Christmas story, just in modern terms."

Annie groaned and shook her head. "Go on, Mr. Brown," she said with reluctance.

Harvey looked around at the others there. Sheriff Hughes, Wilfred, and Mr. Mulligan sat off to one side, going over their lines one last time before it was their turn.

Elsie giggled. "At least our lines are straight from the Good Book. I'd hate to have Joseph and Mary ride into an Indian village and find not one spare teepee to be had."

Bowen laughed. It earned him a "shhhh!" from the Reverend and Mrs. King. He stifled it as best he could. They were seated in a pew in the back of the church until it was time for them to take their turn on the stage. "Maybe the three wise men should be wearing their hats and bandanas."

"That'll never work! The innkeeper might mistake them for outlaws and toss them out!"

Bowen's smile suddenly faded. The heat of shame crept into his cheeks, and he turned his face away.

"Is something wrong?"

"No, nothing." He cleared his throat and rubbed a hand over his face before he turned back to her. She was all beauty and innocence. What would she think if she knew he'd run with several outlaw gangs? Granted, he'd never actually committed a crime – every time he tried, the opposite would happen and he would wind up saving the day. But would that matter to her? The intent to do wrong had driven him – was still driving him, every time he thought about that new safe – and where had it gotten him?

Right. Here.

Bowen's eyes widened at the thought. Right here in front of this lovely creature who looked at him as if he was some sort of hero. But he knew he wasn't, no matter what all the newspapers between Philadelphia and the Grand Tetons said about him. He closed his eyes briefly as if opening them again would make his past disappear.

When he did, Elsie was still looking at him, her head cocked to one side in curiosity. "What are you thinking?" she asked softly.

"About you," escaped his lips without a second thought.

She blushed and smiled shyly. "I hope you're not thinking of strapping me to a travois and pulling me along behind you to that Indian village." She smiled then – a wide, mischievous smile.

Bowen had to cover his mouth with both hands to keep from laughing. She was so utterly adorable, he almost couldn't stand it! Good Lord, but he wanted to kiss her – if for nothing else than to wipe the look of mischief from her face! And preferably replace it with one of passion.

What was so different about her? He hadn't exactly been an angel over the last few years when it came to women, and he'd been with some beautiful ones. Yet, at that very moment, sitting in front of Elsie, he realized none of them could possibly compare to her. She had one thing missing from all the rest – a true zest for life.

"I think we're next," she told him softly.

Bowen couldn't help himself. He leaned forward and bent his face close to hers. "I think you're right."

"Ahem …" Bowen and Elsie both looked up to find Sheriff Hughes standing in the pew in front of them. "Your turn."

Bowen sat up straight. "Yes, we're coming." He stood, pulling Elsie up along with him, and led her from the pew and up the aisle. It wasn't until he got to the front of the church that he realized he was holding her hand again. He looked down and slowly let it go, then realized the Rev. King and his wife had noticed. Oh dear. He tried to be nonchalant, raising his hand up and rubbing his chin a few times. Elsie, also realizing their peril, took a step to the side away from him.

The Rev. King smiled, winked at his wife and said, "Let's proceed, shall we? Now, as you two are playing Joseph and Mary, it's important to convey to the audience that you are husband and wife."

Bowen's eyes widened, while Elsie's lit up like a Christmas tree. "C-convey?" Bowen asked slowly.

"Yes. Hold her hand, stare deeply into her eyes when you speak your lines to her, that sort of thing," the Reverend explained with a grin.

Bowen's brow furrowed. Good grief! How was he going to survive this? "Is that in the script?"

"It doesn't have to be in the script. Everyone knows Joseph and Mary loved each other."

"Are they gonna kiss?" Wilfred yelled from the back of the church.

Bowen turned and faced the cross on the wall behind him. "Oh, dear Lord …" *Can You make this any harder on a man?*

"That's a good idea, Wilfred – maybe they should."

"Josiah King!" Annie admonished. "You can't have them kissing on stage in the church!"

"Why not? Perhaps they should kiss after Jesus is born, while Mary is holding Him in her arms, Joseph at her side looking down upon Him. Yes, I think that would be a very touching scene."

"Josiah …" Annie warned him.

He turned to his wife. "What's wrong with it?"

"It's not *proper.*"

"What's not proper about it? Seems perfectly natural to me."

"I don't mind," Elsie said, perhaps a little too excitedly.

The three wise men – or as Bowen was beginning to think of them, the three wiseacres – burst into laughter in the back of the church. "Awww, go ahead," Sheriff Hughes said. "Let 'em kiss!"

"What could it hurt?" Patrick Mulligan added. "The lass said she didn't mind!"

Annie turned in the pew and glared at the three men in the back. "You hush!" She faced the front again and looked at Elsie. "You really don't mind if it's included? It seems so, so ... well, what will people think?"

"He could ... kiss her on the cheek," the Reverend said in an attempt at compromise.

"What if I don't want to kiss her?" Bowen suddenly blurted.

Elsie's face fell, her eyes downcast. Bowen wanted to kick himself. He'd just hurt her out of his nervousness. It was as if he could feel her heart sink to the floor.

"What man wouldn't want to kiss her?" A voice spoke from one side of the stage.

Everyone turned to look at the newcomer. "Ah, welcome, Your Grace," the Rev. King said.

Bowen looked from the preacher to the man standing behind the organ and back again. "Jesus?"

"Not quite, but close," the new arrival retorted.

The three wiseacres in the back burst out laughing again.

"If you three can't keep it together back there, then go practice someplace else!" Annie scolded.

"I gotta get back to work anyway," Sheriff Hughes said. "I'm glad I signed up for this – it's just what the town needs." He stood. "Coming, Wilfred?"

"Oh, yes – I need to get back to work as well."

"Work? Sure 'n begorrah, you two are gonna go play checkers!" Mulligan snorted.

"Well, that's work!" Sheriff Hughes shot back. "Hard work, too!"

Patrick Mulligan got up and followed the two men down the aisle, through the doors and outside, arguing with them the whole time. In the meantime, the man behind the organ stepped away from it and approached Bowen and Elsie. "Good afternoon. I don't believe we've met."

Another Englishman. This must be the eldest Cooke brother Mr. Van Cleet had spoken of. Bowen took the hand the man offered. "Bowen Drake," he said. "And this is my wife ... er, ah ... Elsie Waller."

Josiah King snorted into the script in his hand, while his wife Annie giggled at Bowen's slip.

Duncan Cooke raised an eyebrow in amusement and smiled. "An understandable mistake. She is, after all, your wife in the play. And as I said before, who wouldn't want to kiss her – or marry her, for that matter?" He bowed to Elsie, took one of her hands in his own, raised it to his lips and brushed it with a kiss.

Elsie blushed crimson and took an involuntary step towards Bowen. "It's a ... a pleasure to meet you," she stammered.

Duncan smiled at the action as he let go of her hand. "And I you. Cozette has told me all about you. I do hope you've found our little town to your liking, Miss Waller."

She nodded enthusiastically. "Oh yes, I love it here! I'm so glad I came."

"And you, Mr. Drake – have you found Clear Creek to your liking?"

Bowen took a step closer to Elsie, putting himself right behind her. "Yes, I have."

Duncan smiled again then turned on his heel to face the preacher. "Am I late?"

"Not at all. I'll have to find something tall enough for you to stand on, so you're above everyone else."

"What part are you playing, Mr. Cooke? Can I call you that?" Elsie asked. "Isn't there something else one calls a duke?"

He smiled. "In this case, I do believe I'm God. Or is it an angel of some sort? I'm not exactly sure what I've been cast as. But as to how to address me, I've been told that 'Your Grace' is the formal term. Frankly, it makes no difference to me."

"I hear you're to leave for London in the spring. I would think you'd want to get used to being addressed properly." Bowen said. Duncan Cooke certainly had the regal bearing of a duke that was for sure, yet it was hard to combine the title with the towering man who was dressed as a simple cowhand.

"Yes, there are those who concur with you on that, Mr. Drake – and remind me of it all too often," Duncan said flatly.

"You don't like being addressed as befits your new station?"

"Coming from the townspeople of Clear Creek, it does feel a little odd. What kind of duke is no match for a woman with a ladle, for example? Mrs. Dunnigan should be knighted for slaying dragons. I'm afraid I can't compare to her heroics."

Bowen and Elsie both stared at him. They'd heard tales around town of the Cooke brothers and their heroics, and a few tales of the other townsfolk. "What indeed," Bowen finally said.

Duncan looked at him and smiled. "Tell me, where were you educated?"

Bowen's eyes slammed open in surprise. He hadn't realized how easily he'd slipped into a much more formal speech pattern until he started speaking with a noble. Should he tell him? Would it hurt at this point? What if they found out about his … *gift*? "Um … back east."

"Where 'back east' exactly?"

Bowen swallowed, and stole a quick glance at the Reverend and his wife. He'd given the same answer to Mr. Van Cleet, who hadn't pressed him further, but that clearly wasn't going to be the case with Duncan Cooke. "Harvard, actually," he finally said, his shoulders slumping.

Elsie gasp, as did Annie. Bowen knew they were both wondering what on Earth a Harvard man was doing way out west. Elsie looked especially shocked and, Bowen sensed, saddened. In fact, it looked like her eyes were filling with tears. But why – was she sad or glad to find he was an educated man?

"Do tell? I say, whatever did you study there?"

Oh, he might as well get it over with. "Natural philosophy, mostly." Which was true as far as it went – you needed a lot of science credits to move on to the medical school …

"Natural philosophy?" Duncan exclaimed. "Pray tell, but what is a Harvard graduate of *natural philosophy* doing here in the back of the beyond? Were you heading to Oregon City to teach?"

"I … ahhh … not exactly, no …"

"Preacher Jo!" Willie the stagecoach driver called as he burst through the doors of the church. "Come quick!"

The Rev. King immediately stood. "What's wrong?"

"It's Doc Waller! He needs ya right away!"

"Whatever for?" Annie asked as she too stood.

"Best you come too, ma'am, and you, Miss Waller – 'specially you!"

"What is it?" Elsie asked alarmed. "What's happened?"

"It's yer Grandma, miss – she done collapsed! Doc can't get 'er to wake up!"

Elsie screamed and fled down the aisle. Duncan Cooke was close behind, as were the preacher and his wife as they jumped to their feet. Bowen was the only one who didn't move. He stood, his hands balled into fists as he watched them race for the church doors and follow Willie out into the cold.

The women didn't even bother to grab their coats on the way out. Elsie would be cold. He needed to make sure she kept warm ...

The thought was lost as his mind waged war. *Don't! Don't help them! If you do, you'll just be sucked back into that world again! The world of liars and hypocrites you've run so far to escape!*

But he knew he had to help. It went far beyond his conscience; it was an overwhelming urge, a need that drove him. When it hit him, he felt like he was woven into something much bigger than himself, a tapestry the size of humanity. Should he refuse to do his part, it would be incomplete. He could no more fight it than keep the sun from rising.

Bowen took one step forward, then another. Before he knew it, he was running out the church doors and into the cold. A light snow had begun to fall, and he belatedly realized he'd failed to grab his own coat as well as Elsie's.

Too late now. His calling had taken over.

He followed their footprints in the snow all the way to the livery stable. Several men had come out of the hotel and were quickly making their way down the street. He expected them to run straight to the Wallers' home, but instead they turned and ran toward the mercantile. Then he noticed Elsie and the others following Willie up the mercantile steps and inside. The doors had barely shut before the workers, with Mr. Van Cleet among them, reached the building, went in and closed the doors behind them.

Bowen stopped at the foot of the steps and caught his breath, swallowed. He stared at the twin pine wreaths on the doors with their matching red bows as he tried to brace himself.

He knew what was coming. It was part of the reason

he'd kept moving west, why he'd joined one gang after another, why he'd been thrown out of one gang after another. It didn't matter who he was with or where, his *gift* followed. It never left him, and there were times like now when he couldn't fight it – it seemed to act of its own accord. He was merely the vessel that carried it to some unworthy wretch upon whom it would pour itself out and ultimately … heal them.

He shook with cold. He hated being cold now, ever since it had almost killed him. Yet he almost longed to be frozen to that spot. Because after this the people of Clear Creek would know, and they would never treat him the same again.

But he had no choice. He knew that.

Bowen closed his eyes, took another deep breath, climbed the steps and opened the door.

Nine

ELSIE KNELT NEXT TO GRANDMA, who lay inert on the floor, Grandpa on her other side. "What's wrong with her?" she asked through her tears.

"I'm thinking it's her heart," Grandpa said, his voice trembling. He wiped away a tear of his own. "Back up, people – give her some breathing room!"

The crowd of men gathered around took a few steps back.

It was the strangest thing, but Elsie could swear she *felt* Bowen before he came through the mercantile door. She'd wondered why he hadn't left the church with the rest of them – in fact, she didn't realize he'd stayed behind until she arrived at Dunnigan's. She'd turned to look at him before she entered, hoping for the reassurance of his presence. But he wasn't there. Until now.

Grandpa Waller continued to examine his wife as he fought against his own rising panic. Preacher Jo quietly knelt down beside him. "Do you want us to help you take her home?"

Grandpa sniffed and wiped at his nose. "I ... I suppose ..." He looked helplessly at Preacher Jo. "I can't lose her, do ya hear me? I can't ..."

Elsie's tears ran freely down her face. Was Grandpa saying what she thought he was? Was Grandma dying? She closed her eyes and raised her face to the ceiling. *Please, Lord, don't let her die! I've lost so many already! I know that's selfish of me, but I don't care!*

Someone knelt beside her. Bowen! "Her heart?"

Elsie nodded. "Th-that's what Grandpa thinks."

Bowen looked down at Grandma Waller. Her face was deathly pale, her breathing almost non-existent. He closed his eyes – and he could feel the weakness of her body, the numbness in her mind, the slow steady crawl of death as it crept its way into her.

Unable to help himself, he let his God-given gift flow.

As with all the others, he simply reached out and touched Grandma Waller. It never mattered where. In this case it was her leg, since that's what he was closest to. Then he waited for the inevitable to happen.

He sighed as memories came back. The last person he'd touched like this was an "outlaw" with a gunshot wound – actually just a child, fourteen at the oldest, the son of the gang leader. But after he'd touched him, the bleeding suddenly stopped. The gang leader had stared at Bowen as if he was the devil himself, and promptly pistol-whipped him. When he came to, he found the gang had left him tied to a tree, taken his money and ammo, and left only his nag of a horse; the same horse that had brought him to Clear Creek a week ago. That's gratitude for you. But over the years, he'd learned a thing or two about covering his tracks.

A preacher he'd met along the trail told him he had a gift of "miracles and healing," which admittedly would serve him well as a doctor. But he always felt more like a carnival freak when folks put two and two together and realized what he'd done. He knew there was no way it was *him* doing this – he was just the vessel the Almighty was using. He really wished God had given him a choice in the matter, but He hadn't.

And why hadn't He dumped this gift on him *before* his mother died? The very thought upset him to no end, and left him just as upset at God as he was at his earthly father. Sometimes he didn't know which one he was angry with more.

However, the Almighty was too busy with him at the moment to let him argue the point – not that He ever did anyway. "I think we should take her to your home," he whispered to Elsie. "She'll be more comfortable there." He sighed again wearily, sat back on his heels and pulled his hand away.

"Are you all right?" Elsie asked softly.

"Yes," Bowen whispered. It was always hard to talk afterward; the overwhelming presence of something so powerful, so infinite, always left him feeling like a schoolroom blackboard that had been freshly erased. That was part of why he constantly ran from it.

But should he? Why couldn't he be doing what the Rev. King, "Preacher Jo," did? Or for that matter, go back to doctoring? When he thought on all the good he could be used for, it astounded him. But there was still that fear (often justified) of people's reactions when they found out he was different. There was his resentment toward doctors, his father and professors especially. And there was his frustration at seemingly having no say in his own life …

Speaking of "Preacher Jo" … he looked up and saw the clergyman staring open-mouthed at him. Oh dear …

Thankfully, it was then that Grandma Waller stirred. "Sarah!" Doc Waller cried. "Sarah, can ya hear me?"

She opened her eyes slowly, her face still deathly pale. "Land sakes," she hissed. "What in … in tarnation are y'all looking at?"

Doc Waller's body shook with suppressed sobs. "Sarah!" he cried as he gathered her into his arms and helped her sit up. "I thought … I thought …"

"You thought what? What's wrong with everyone? What happened?"

Mrs. Dunnigan, quiet all this time, stepped through the crowd. "You fainted."

"Fainted?" Doc looked up at her, one eyebrow raised in question. Mrs. Dunnigan shrugged. She had probably been the one who'd sent for Preacher Jo. But she also didn't want him worrying Grandma. Crotchety, maybe, and stubborn as a mule, but Irene Dunnigan wasn't stupid. "Oh, yes! It's a plumb miracle you didn't hit your head on the way down."

"It's a plumb miracle indeed," Preacher Jo said softly as he took one of Grandma's hands. "Do you think you can stand?"

Grandma looked at the faces around her. "Seems to me, a little faint is causing a mighty big stir."

"Can't be too careful when you're our age, Sarah," Irene Dunnigan huffed.

The mercantile doors flew open, and a huge man strode through the crowd and went straight to Grandma. "Is she all right? I heard …" he said, then suddenly noticed Grandma Waller sitting up on the floor. "You are all right!"

"Of course I'm all right!" Grandma scolded, her voice stronger now. "Why wouldn't I be?"

Bowen and Elsie both stared at the newcomer. He was huge and powerfully built, with a funny accent – German, or maybe Norwegian.

"Because …," the big man began, then noticed Mrs. Dunnigan's warning glare. "*Ach*, I … must have heard wrong. You look perfectly fine. May I escort you home?"

"Andel, child," Grandma answered with a smile. "Since when do you have to ask?"

The giant smiled, gently scooped Grandma Waller up

in his massive arms and set her on her feet. She looked small next to him, but then, almost anyone would. "Doc, I will take her home and up to your room. Is there anything else you need?"

Doc Waller took a deep breath as he also stood. "No, Andel – helping me get her settled will be enough. I … I …" He looked at the people around him, took in the concern and relief on their faces. "Thank you, all of you. I know you were praying. I felt it." He nodded a few times before he followed the man called Andel out the mercantile doors.

Elsie finally stood, her eyes wide as she stared after them. "Did you see that – how she acted like it was nothing? Just a faint, like Mrs. Dunnigan said."

"Maybe that's all it was," Bowen suggested as he rose. "It happens to people her age."

"But Grandpa said it was her heart, just before you got here. That it must've given out on her. They sent for Preacher Jo because…"

"It was a faint, missy!" Mrs. Dunnigan interjected. "Nothing more. Now go on home and see to your grandma."

"But Grandpa said …"

"Your grandfather was wrong, I guess," Bowen told her, and shrugged.

"I suppose," she said softly. But she didn't sound convinced.

Bowen took her arm and placed it on his. "Let me walk you home," he said.

She nodded, and they left the mercantile together.

Preacher Jo reached down and pulled his wife to her feet as the men dispersed to head back to whatever they were doing before they'd heard Grandma was in trouble. He watched most of them file out before he took his wife into his arms. "Did you feel that?" he whispered against her hair.

"Yes," she whispered back.

"I've felt it before, a long time ago. When we were both young. Do you remember, that time ..."

Annie looked up at him. "The time the outlaws forced you to shoot my brother?"

"Yes. I knew the Lord wasn't going to let you die, that He was there protecting you."

"God does have a way of making good come out of evil, that's for sure." Annie said.

The incident had happened years ago. Annie had been all of fifteen, Josiah a hired hand on her parents' farm. Her ma and pa had died the year before, and her brother Sam and Josiah were trying to keep the farm going as best they could. But Sam had gotten into some bad habits with liquor and cards. His luck ran dry in a poker game, and when the men he'd played with showed up at the farm to collect, he didn't have the money. In retaliation, they'd forced Josiah to do the unthinkable.

Yet God had taken the years between then and now to mold her and Josiah into the people they were today. That, in itself, was a pure miracle.

Josiah and Annie looked at each other, knowing they had just witnessed another one.

Bowen stood just inside the Wallers' front door. "Are you going to be all right?" he asked Elsie.

"Yes," she replied numbly. "I still don't understand how ..."

The door to the bedroom at the top of the stairs opened. The giant Andel descended, Doc Waller right behind him. "Elsie, fetch Mr. Berg some coffee, will you?"

She nodded and quickly went down the hall to the kitchen. Bowen watched her go, then turned his attention to the huge man now standing in front of him. He was a good head taller than Bowen, who wasn't by any measure short, and much broader too. "Good evening."

Andel looked past him to the window by the door. It was growing dark outside. "That it is. You must be the man Elsie Waller saved."

That again? Was there anyone in this town who *didn't* think of it that way? Well, it could be worse – at least they weren't talking about what had happened with Grandma. Yet. "Yes, she saved me."

The huge man extended a hand. "I'm Andel Berg. August tells me you are keeping an eye on Doc and Grandma's little Elsie. I'm glad to hear it."

Bowen took the man's hand to shake it, and almost got his own lost in it. "Er, yes. It seems a wise precaution to take, with women being so scarce here."

Mr. Berg eyed him carefully. "Yes, it is. Keep it up, will you? I myself prefer to stay home with my wife, now that winter has set in."

Bowen felt a sudden pang of jealousy, but dismissed it when Elsie came down the hall carrying two cups of coffee. She handed one to Mr. Berg, and one to him. He took it gratefully. Having left his coat at the church, the short walk to the Wallers' home was all it took to chill him to the bone.

"Do you want some coffee, too, Grandpa?" Elsie asked him.

"I'll get some in a minute, honey. Have I introduced you to Mr. Berg?"

Elsie stared up at the giant, who was taking a sip of the hot brew she'd given him. "No. I'm sure I would remember if you had."

Doc let out a small chuckle. "That's what most folks say about Mr. Berg. Andel, this is my ... well, actually she's my third cousin, but she calls me Grandpa."

Mr. Berg smiled. "I hope you like it here in Clear Creek."

"Yes, I ... I do like it here."

Bowen took a step forward. It was all he could do to keep from taking her in his arms. She was frightened, he could tell, frightened and overwhelmed. He knew the feeling well.

"Why don't you and Mr. Drake go sit a spell in the parlor, honey?" Doc told her. "I'm gonna speak with Mr. Berg here a moment."

"Yes, Grandpa." Elsie took Bowen by the hand and unceremoniously pulled him into the parlor with her. He glanced over his shoulder at the other two men, but Doc Waller and Mr. Berg were already heading back up the stairs. What was going on? Why was he leaving him alone with her? He probably wanted to check on his wife again, but leaving his charge un-chaperoned at the same time?

Bowen turned to Elsie just as she buried her face in her hands. "Hey now, what's this?"

"I can't help it," she sobbed. "I know something was terribly wrong with Grandma, I know it! And to see her sit up and talk like nothing had happened ..."

Bowen felt dread drop into his gut like a brick. Were there others as upset by the old woman's miraculous recovery? If so, would he have to run again? It wouldn't be the first time, but that didn't make it any easier. "Elsie..."

She sniffed and looked up at him. "I'm sorry, it's just that ... that ..."

Bowen didn't even bother to try to stop himself. He set his coffee cup down on a nearby table, took her in his arms, and held her. She buried her face in his chest and sobbed. "It's all right, sweetheart. Your grandmother's fine now. I'm sure she'll be herself in no time."

She sniffed back her tears, wiped her eyes with the palm of her hand, and looked up at him. "Do you ... do you really think so?" she said in between a series of small hiccups.

Lord, he wanted to kiss her! But he didn't dare. "I know so."

"How do you know?"

"Because she's too tough to be otherwise. Now dry your eyes before your grandfather comes down here and thinks I've done something to make you cry."

"Oh, he'd never think that. I cry at the drop of a hat."

Bowen put a finger under her chin and lifted her face to his. "You do?"

She nodded and sniffed some more.

Bowen smiled. "Well, then I must say you're just the prettiest bucket of tears I ever did see."

That made her smile. She wiped her eyes again. "Would you like to sit down?"

He smiled as he took her hand and led her to the settee. They sat and she primly folded her hands in her lap. "You're going to stay, aren't you?" she suddenly asked him.

"Stay?"

"In Clear Creek."

Now, what prompted her to ask that out of the blue? "I ... well, I ..." How was he to answer that? He glanced briefly at the ceiling. *You're not going to make this easy on me, are you, Lord?* "I haven't decided."

Her eyes widened. "What is there to decide? You like

it here, don't you?"

Bowen had learned over the last few years that the Almighty had quite a sense of humor when it came to him. "Of course, but ... I hadn't really thought about what I'd do past the winter ..."

"Until now?" she asked hopefully.

Bowen suddenly felt like taking his coffee cup from the table and throwing it at the ceiling.

I've brought you here for a reason.

Bowen froze. The voice of reason again. Blast it.

"I hear Clear Creek is beautiful in the spring," she quickly added.

Bowen looked at her. Clear Creek wasn't the only thing that was beautiful. She was, undeniably so, and he felt something then that he hadn't felt in years. Hope. Hope that at last his life would straighten out, that he'd finally found a place where he could belong, that his heart would heal from the bitterness he'd let fester against his father, against his teachers, against doctors, against God, against the world ...

Besides, the poison he'd concocted for his father and others to drink and die from – it wasn't killing them. It was killing him. That was how un-forgiveness usually worked.

"Beautiful," he whispered. Just looking at her gave him hope.

"Yes, with the spring flowers on the prairie and all ..."

He scooted a few inches closer. "I suppose I could con-sider it."

"And the town's planning a big send-off for Duncan Cooke and the others leaving for Europe ..."

His head bent down as hers tilted back. This wasn't something he should be doing – but then, he would've said that about laying his hand on Grandma Waller too.

"So I heard," he replied, his voice husky.

Any time now, Doc Waller and that giant would come down the stairs, probably just as he kissed her – that's usually how his life worked. Then Mr. Berg would pound him into paste and shovel him out the door. *Think of the pain, Bowen!*

But this voice wasn't the voice of reason, nor the Almighty's, just the voice of self- preservation, one he didn't listen to very much. Including now. He took Elsie in his arms again as his eyes fixed on her mouth. "London should be very beautiful in the spring."

"I … I almost wish I could go with them," she gasped.

"Do you now?" he said as his forehead met hers. Their lips were maybe an inch apart. "And what would you do in London?"

"Not what I can do here."

"What can you do in Clear Creek that you can't do in London?" he asked as he heard something. Was it the door at the top of the stairs?

"This," she breathed, and without warning brought her lips up to his.

Ten

BOWEN WAS NO INNOCENT IN this respect; he had kissed his fair share of women over the years. But knew in that moment that Elsie Waller was new at it. Sure, she initiated it, but she was clumsy at best. He was actually glad for it – had he initiated the kiss as he'd wanted to, he wasn't sure he'd be able to stop.

As it was, he didn't have to worry about stopping. Mr. Berg took care of that for him.

Bowen yelped in surprise when the giant's two huge hands grabbed him by the shoulders and yanked him off the settee. He knew he shouldn't have let her kiss him for as long as she did, but Elsie had put her hands on either side of his face and he couldn't really pull away. Not without seeming quite rude. Besides, he didn't want it to stop, and in a split-second moment of insanity had decided to face the consequences and take it like a man.

Of course, now the consequences were hitting home – specifically, hitting his shoulder, upon which Mr. Berg still had an iron-clad grip even though he was now standing up and several feet from Elsie.

"What in tarnation's going on in here?" Doc Waller demanded.

Mr. Berg glared down at Bowen but didn't say a word.

Elsie suddenly stood. "I kissed him, Grandpa," she declared.

Bowen did a double-take. Out of the corner of his eye he could see Mr. Berg doing the same.

"*You* kissed *him*?" Doc Waller asked, astounded.

"Yes, I did." Elsie said as she stood her ground. "He had nothing to do with it."

Bowen wanted to say, *well, not nothing* … but decided such wit would not be appropriate at the moment.

"What the …" Doc spun on Bowen. "Is this true? Or is she protecting your sorry hide?"

Bowen looked at Elsie who stood proudly now, chin up, arms crossed. It was all he could do to keep from smiling. The girl had spunk, he had to give her that. "Yes, sir. I'm afraid it is."

"Elsie!" Doc exclaimed. "What's gotten into you, girl?"

"I suppose now you'll demand he marry me or some such thing," she said matter-of-factly.

Bowen's eyes widened. How badly *did* she want him to stay in Clear Creek? Good grief, what *was* she doing? He looked at Mr. Berg just in time to see him slap a hand over his face and let it slide down to his chin, clearly trying to keep from laughing.

"What are you expecting, a shotgun wedding?" Doc quipped.

"If we must, I'm willing to go through with it." Elsie said dramatically.

Mr. Berg sounded like he was choking.

"Oh, for Pete's sake, girl! There ain't gonna be no shotgun wedding!" Doc admonished.

"What?" Elsie asked, shocked. "But why not? I kissed him, for crying out loud!" She pointed at Bowen and stomped her foot. "I, I, I compromised him!"

That did it! Mr. Berg actually doubled over, he was laughing so hard.

Bowen, still trying to figure out what was going on, was at least relieved he didn't have that huge paw on his shoulder anymore. He'd heard Andel Berg had worked as a blacksmith, and now felt rather sorry for the horses.

Doc Waller looked from Elsie to Bowen and back again. "Oh, honey, I see what this is all about," he said with a shake of his head. "You always were a little unconventional, just like your ma. But don't you think Mr. Drake has a say as to whether or not he courts ya?"

Elsie turned to Bowen, her eyes hopeful. God, but she was beautiful, even when she was acting silly. But she didn't think she wasn't being silly … she was … she …

Oh, dear Lord. Was she in love with him? Could it be? By some slim chance, could it actually be? Or was it some odd notion that made her think she had to protect him because she'd saved his life? He knew it happened to men all the time when it came to women they'd rescued. Were the girl's protective instincts that strong?

Bowen suddenly smiled. All in all, it was rather flattering.

"I know what this man needs!" Mr. Berg suddenly declared. "You talk some sense into your granddaughter, Doc, while I escort Mr. Drake back to the hotel."

Elsie was almost in hysterics. "But, but … isn't anybody going to demand he make an honest woman out of me?"

"Seems to me it's the other way around," Doc said flatly.

Elsie looked as if she was going to cry again. "But …"

"No buts," Doc said. "There ain't gonna be no shotgun wedding! What is the matter with you, carrying on like this? I know that what happened to your grandma upset you, but she's upstairs resting all comfortable-like. Now, settle yourself down before I send you to your room!"

Elsie swallowed hard, her face now flushed with embarrassment. She looked at Bowen then, her lips tight, and said, "I'm so sorry. I've just made a complete fool of myself."

Bowen walked over to Elsie. "I understand. Don't worry, I …" He leaned over to whisper in her ear. "I would have kissed you, you know. You just beat me to it."

He pulled back to see her eyes were wide and shining, her cheeks red. "I'm sorry," she replied. Then she ran from the room, up the stairs, and disappeared into her bedroom.

Doc sighed in relief and scratched the back of his neck. "I apologize for this, Mr. Drake, I don't' know what's gotten into that girl lately. Maybe it's because she just lost her real grandpa. That's why she came to live here. She's a dreamer, that one — and full of more curiosity than should be allowed."

Bowen too sighed. "It's all right. She's probably distraught over what happened to her grandmother. I'm sure she'll be fine." He looked at the stairs. "She's really quite charming."

Doc shook his head. "She's spirited, that's for sure. Ted and I used to think it too much for her own good."

Bowen smiled. "When the right man comes along, it'll probably settle her down."

Doc and Mr. Berg both looked at him. "And are you the right man, Mr. Drake?" Mr. Berg asked him.

"Me? Oh, well … I …"

"I saw what happened," Mr. Berg said. "She may have started the kiss, but you finished it. There are those who would force you to marry her."

"Now wait a minute," Bowen said. "What would you know of it?"

Mr. Berg smiled broadly as Doc began laughing. "Trust me when I say, I know more about shotgun weddings than you might think." He put a tree limb of an arm around Bowen, then yanked him close. "And as I said before, I know just what you need."

"Umph!" Bowen found himself barely able to breathe. "What might that be?"

"What say you and I go down to the saloon and have ourselves a piece of pie?"

Doc laughed even louder.

Bowen was totally confused at this point. "Pie?"

"Indeed, Mr. Drake. Mrs. Dunnigan's pies are a well-known cure-all for just about everything. Isn't that right, Doc?"

Doc couldn't answer. Doc could barely breathe, he was guffawing so hard.

Bowen felt his ribs creak as the giant kept him locked in a steel grip, almost lifting him off the ground as he turned toward the door. He released Bowen long enough to put on his hat, only to grab him again and shove him out.

Bowen had no idea what all this pie business was about, but did know one thing. Elsie Waller and the word "marriage" in the same sentence hadn't scared him as much as he thought it would. What did, however, was what Elsie might do if she could prove he had anything to do with her grandmother's sudden recovery.

Even though the normal course of events with he and women appeared to be changing, would she still be interested in him if she knew that he was, for lack of a better term, a freak?

Elsie listened to the men through the door. She'd opened it just a crack, wondering if Bowen would say anything that would make her feel any better about what she'd done. But all they seemed to be talking about downstairs was … pie?!

Elsie finally closed the door, flung herself on the bed and cried into her pillow. What was she thinking, acting so brazenly? Had she lost her mind? Good God, she'd kissed him! She'd *kissed* Bowen Drake! "Oh Grandma, I'm so sorry; I don't know what came over me."

But Grandma was in the other room, probably asleep by now. For Heaven's sake, what was she doing apologizing to Grandma for anyway? She hadn't seen what happened. But Elsie wished she had. Grandma Waller had fast become a mother figure, and the thought of losing her earlier had about ripped Elsie's heart out. She'd kissed Bowen because she was desperate to hang on to something, *someone* in her life who wouldn't leave her.

"They all leave me," she whispered into the darkness, having never bothered to light the lamp. She got up from the bed and went to stand next to the window. It had stopped snowing, and stars were beginning to appear. "Bowen, I'm so sorry. What must you think of me?"

He would have nothing more to do with her, of course. She'd humiliated herself in front of him, all but thrown herself at him, then tried to keep him in Clear Creek by suggesting a shotgun wedding.

But why?

She looked out the window again, and could see the moon rising. "I'm so sorry," she said to no one in particular. "Why do I do such foolish things? I don't think, don't … take into consideration the consequences. I'm so sorry. For everything … for losing everyone I've ever loved. I … I just didn't want to lose …"

Elsie's eyes widened. "… to lose this man too."

She *was* in love with him!

Elsie turned from the window as fresh tears flowed down her face. "Oh, Mother, I wish you were here to see me. Grandpa Teddy …" She tried to stifle a sob but it was no use. She fell onto the bed and at long last truly grieved the loss of her parents, the grandfather who'd raised her after they died – and in all likelihood, the man she had just come to realize she loved.

Andel Berg dragged Bowen down the street to Mulligan's and shoved him through the doors. Bowen nearly tripped with the momentum, and wondered if this was a normal thing for the giant to do, or if the man had any idea of his own strength. He didn't envy Andel such a thing – the big man likely had no shortage of men wanting to fight him just to say they had, whether they won or not.

"What's brings you in, laddies?" Mr. Mulligan asked from behind the bar as he wiped a glass.

Andel smiled broadly as he shoved Bowen up to the bar. "Pie," was all he said.

The entire bar burst into laughter.

Bowen felt a flicker of worry. He swallowed hard and turned to the men who were, for the most part, just finishing their dinner – Mulligan's saloon was more a restaurant than anything else. Did that explain the pie, then?

"Woman trouble?" Mr. Mulligan asked.

Bowen slowly turned around. Was he talking to him? "Er, no, not really."

Andel slapped him on the back. "Oh, come now, I saw the look on your face. You fancy her – admit it."

"Well, I … ah …do we really need to be discussing

this here?"

"Of course! There are no secrets in Clear Creek!" Andel chortled and slapped Bowen on the back hard enough to send him into the bar and knock the breath out of him. "Bring this man some pie!"

A cheer went up from the rest of the men in the saloon, and Bowen began to feel *very* worried as he fought to get his breath back. Andel grabbed him and pulled him a few feet to a nearby table, where he shoved him into a chair. Mr. Mulligan, in the meantime, had disappeared into the back of the saloon.

"If you got woman trouble, son, a piece of pie will fix you right up!" a man called. "Ain't that right, Andel?"

Andel smiled devilishly. "Yes, that's exactly right."

Bowen couldn't believe it. He actually gulped while men started to gather around the table. Andel sat himself down opposite Bowen and grinned. "Ah … is there something I should know?" Bowen asked. "Because I'm not exactly following any of this…"

He was interrupted by a cheer that went up as Mr. Mulligan came around the bar, several pies balanced on each arm. Bowen took in the looks of anticipation among the men, including Andel's. "What is this all about?!" he asked in panic.

Mr. Mulligan set three pies in front of Bowen, the other three in front of Andel. "What say we show this gent how we eat pie in Clear Creek?" he asked the crowd. Another cheer went up, and more laughter.

Bowen stared at the pies in front of him. "What am I supposed to do with these?"

Andel smiled. "Eat them, of course."

"All three? Are you out of your mind?"

"I hold the record." Andel said proudly.

"For … pie eating? Is that what people do around here

for fun?"

"Not for fun," Andel said. "More for sanity than any-thing, at least where women are concerned." He took a napkin and tucked it under his chin. "Trust me when I say that in the morning, you'll have a much keener sense of how you truly feel about the girl."

Was Andel serious? A pie-eating contest? What kind of a screwy town was this? How was this supposed to help him figure out how he felt about Elsie Waller? But then ... how *did* he feel about Elsie Waller, really?

Bowen watched Andel pick up a pie tin and pull half the pie out of it. He motioned for Bowen to do the same. Mr. Mulligan flipped open a pocket watch and held up a hand.

"Quick! Pick up your pie!" someone yelled at Bowen.

Bowen automatically did so. He couldn't believe he was actually going to do this, but he supposed it beat the alternative. Better to be facing off against Andel Berg with a pie in his hand than a gun – or given the other man's size, bare knuckles.

Now this was how his luck usually ran – oddly. Though some sort of good always came out of it ... for everyone else, that is. He hoped he didn't choke on a bite of pie-crust or suddenly find that the berries didn't agree with him. With his luck, he'd inhale a smattering of cinnamon and fall out of his chair. Stranger things had happened. What he really wanted to know, however, was how he ended up going from being part of a miracle, to stealing (actually, being gifted) a kiss from Elsie Waller, to get-ting roped into a crazy pie-eating contest with a man who looked more like he belonged on a Viking warship than in a nothing town like Clear Creek.

But at this point, he felt a twinge of regret at the thought of leaving this madhouse. Would he still want to go in the spring? More importantly, would he still want to leave Elsie? Who knew what could happen between them over the next few months? Did he dare allow himself to fall in love with her? Could he? Or would she come close to marrying him, then be off like all the rest? She was fast becoming the one woman he didn't want to lose …

Bowen tried to push the thoughts aside as he took in the scene around him – the men surrounding the table; Andel sitting across from him, his pie in hand, ready to go; Mr. Mulligan with his watch in one hand, his other just now making its descent.

"Go!"

He needed a drink, he realized, maybe several. But perhaps, as nutty a notion as it was, a pie-eating contest was the next best thing. Nothing for it, then - he started to wolf down the first half of an apple pie. And sure enough, the cheer of the onlookers, the determined gleam in his opponent's eye across the table, and the sweet taste of apples and cinnamon knocked out any thought of Elsie Waller he might have.

But what was he going to feel like in the morning after a night of frenzied pie-eating?

He decided he'd just have to wait and find out.

Eleven

ELSIE FIDGETED IN THE PEW at church the next day. There was no sign of Bowen Drake. There was no sign of Andel Berg, either, and she was starting to worry about what might have happened to them.

As if able to read her thoughts, Grandpa Waller leaned over and whispered in her ear. "Don't go worrying none about last night. My guess is that Mr. Drake and Mr. Berg ain't feeling too well this morning."

Elsie slowly turned to look at him. "Are you implying that they were *drinking* all night?" she gasped.

Grandpa Waller chuckled. "No, I doubt either of them had a drop. But trust me when I say they ain't feeling too good."

Elsie glanced toward Madeline Berg, who sat across the aisle and up a few rows. Some men in the pew in front of Madeline had turned around and were speaking to her. They looked as if they were doing their best not to laugh. Madeline, meanwhile, looked as if she was doing *her* best to be polite and smile. Her mother was expressionless as she stared straight ahead, while her husband, Mr. Duprie, shook as if chilled. That, or he too was trying not to laugh. What was going on?!

"Good morning!" Preacher Jo called out to the congregation. Elsie faced forward again, her voice joining the cheery "good mornings" the townsfolk echoed back to him.

Preacher Jo smiled and took his place behind the pulpit. "Before we get started this morning, I want to give you an update on Grandma Waller. I don't think there's anyone in town who doesn't know her."

The townsfolk nodded and mumbled their agreement.

"Yesterday, Grandma had a spell in the mercantile and … well, some say she fainted. Doc, he says something different. He seems to think it was her heart."

Murmurs raced through the congregation and a few folks reached over and patted Doc and Elsie on their shoulders in reassurance.

"I say God gave us a reminder that life is too short to worry about the little things. Things like wondering if some other woman in town is a better cook than you. That would be comparing yourself to others."

Mrs. Dunnigan sat next to Elsie and she watched as the older woman's jaw tightened then relaxed. Grandma had told her of a culinary rivalry between Mrs. Dunnigan and Mrs. Upton, the cook from the hotel.

"Or if our new bull is better than our neighbors, or if my horse is bigger and able to pull a plow further. Am I smart enough? Am I pretty enough? Have I got all my teeth?"

The townsfolk laughed at that and a few slapped Willie, the stagecoach driver, on the back.

"Lately, many of you have been worrying if you're good enough to participate in the Christmas play. Well, of course you are! Not everyone can participate, as there are only so many parts and jobs to go around, but certainly for those of you who are participating, there's something you're good at that we can use."

Preacher Jo leaned against the pulpit and looked over the townsfolk for a moment, taking in their attentive faces. "Yesterday during play practice, my wife and I were called away to the mercantile because Doc thought

… well, Doc thought he could use God's help. So God came along."

"Amen!" Harvey Brown called from the back of the church as the townspeople nodded in agreement.

Preacher Jo smiled. "I watched those of you who were at the mercantile yesterday pull together, put aside everything you had going on at that moment, and pray. And I think … no, I *believe* that's when God moved in and healed Sarah Waller."

The townsfolk nodded and murmured their agreement.

"So this week, whether you're going about your daily chores, driving to town, baking, making dinner, whatever it may be, send up a prayer for your neighbor. You just never know if they may be in need."

"Hear, hear!" Doc called out just before he stood. He looked around the congregation and smiled. "Grandma wanted me to thank all of you for your prayers yesterday. I made her stay home this morning to rest, but she'll be up and around in no time and feistier than ever. Oh, and as far as anyone's concerned … *she just fainted*." He put a finger to his lips.

Everyone laughed at that. Most had already heard the story of what happened, and if Doc said it was much more serious than a faint, then it was. But he wasn't about to let Grandma know that; at least not until she could handle the news. Elsie thought it hilarious that the whole town knew, but Doc assured her they wouldn't say a word to Grandma. As far as Grandma was concerned, she'd had a fainting spell, nothing more.

"The power of prayer is a beautiful thing," Preacher Jo said again. "Let's all be sure we do plenty of it for each other. I hear it's going to be a long winter."

Men nodded their agreement, while some of the

women in attendance whispered to each other.

"In the meantime, we're going to have a Christmas play come Christmas Eve!" Preacher Jo announced as he threw both arms out to his sides.

A cheer went up.

Preacher Jo smiled, laughed, then motioned to Madeline Berg, who quietly got up and went to the organ. "Let us take out our hymnals, shall we?"

Everyone reached for a hymnal, everyone but Elsie. She sniffed back a tear as she suddenly remembered something from the day before. True, the townspeople had been praying when Elsie got there – it was one of the reasons she'd wanted to see Bowen's face before she looked at the floor. She knew that's where she'd find Grandma and didn't know what to expect other than a prone body, not even whether she would be dead or alive. She certainly didn't expect the look of anguish on Grandpa Waller's face when she'd arrived. But there it was, and that more than anything else had told her the true situation.

But when Bowen arrived, everything in the room changed. Yes, they had all begun to pray, silently or in quiet whispers. Still, when Bowen Drake came into the mercantile, it was as if a peace and calm came with him. She knew he was there without looking for him, and when he knelt beside her his face was serene despite what was happening. All she knew at the time was that she was glad for it, needed it. That peace seemed to wrap around her like a blanket, and in that moment she knew Grandma would be all right.

So why then, when it came to pass, was she so astounded by it? She'd witnessed the hand of the Almighty move yesterday! Doc told her last night it was a miracle, and she'd believed him. So why was it that she could ask God to heal Grandma, watch Him do it, then struggle with the fact that He did? Had she believed that God couldn't do it? And was that why she kissed Bowen, to distract herself from having to face her own unbelief?

Elsie listened to the townsfolk sing the first hymn of the morning. Perhaps she should stay after church and speak with Preacher Jo, or his wife Annie. She needed to sort out her feelings and understand what they all meant. If she didn't know any better, she'd say Bowen had something to do with Grandma's miraculous healing yesterday. After all, nothing had happened until he entered the room, knelt down beside her and touched Grandma's leg.

Come to think of it, the look on his face when he did had been like nothing she'd ever seen before: peace, serenity, and yet sadness too. Why was that? And was that when she lost her heart to him?

Elsie closed her eyes as she joined in the song. Yes, it most definitely was.

But what good did that do her now? After her … slatternly behavior yesterday, he likely wouldn't want anything to do with her. In fact, she wondered if she should tell Preacher Jo and Annie that she couldn't do the play. Surely he wouldn't want to perform with her now after she'd acted like such a fool. Oh, heavens, didn't they have a rehearsal this afternoon? If Bowen wasn't in church this morning, would he even be at the rehearsal later?

Her panic was building. She would have to face him – oh, the humiliation of it all! She glanced around, wondering if any of the townspeople knew what she'd done. But how could they? Grandpa wouldn't say anything, and she was sure Grandma didn't know about it yet.

She released her breath at the end of the hymn. What

was she going to do?

Well, the answer was clear, and there was no help for it. She was just going to have to deal with Bowen Drake, face to face. She closed her eyes against the thought; no sooner had she fallen in love then she botched it up.

Ignoring the liturgy, Elsie closed her eyes and folded her hands. With all of Preacher Jo's talk about prayer this morning, she'd do well to start doing some praying of her own.

"More tea?" Annie asked.

Elsie smiled and nodded. They were seated in the small office located off to one side of the main platform of the church. Elsie sat on one side of the desk, Annie King on the other. She watched Annie pour, then offer her the sugar. Elsie took a small spoonful and stirred it into her tea.

"What's on your mind, Elsie?" Annie asked. "You seem troubled. Is this about Grandma?"

"Oh, no," Elsie said. "I mean, yes … well, it has something to do with her, I suppose."

Annie set her cup and saucer down. "How can I help you?"

"It's rather personal, you see, and I don't think I should bother Grandma with it right now."

Annie smiled at her. "Go on."

Elsie did her best not to squirm in her chair. "So much has happened since I've been here … and I have all these feelings of late, some of which I'm trying to understand."

"Do you miss your old home?"

"A little, but that's not it."

Annie smiled and nodded for her to continue.

Elsie squared her shoulders. "I ... I do believe I'm in love."

"In love?" Annie calmly asked as she picked up her cup.

"You don't sound surprised."

"Should I be?"

"Well, I am!"

Annie laughed at that. "Does this have anything to do with Bowen Drake?"

Elsie stared at the preacher's wife as words started to form on her lips but no sound came out.

"I've seen the way he looks at you," Annie said, filling the awkward silence.

"Looks ... at *me*?"

"And vice versa."

"Oh, dear. I hadn't really noticed. Okay, so that's not entirely true, but it seems to me that two people would need more time to fall in love."

"I fell in love with my husband the moment I saw him."

"You *did*?"

"Yes."

Elsie thought about that a moment then asked, "How long after the two of you met did you marry?"

"Years. I was thirteen when we first met – far too young."

"Oh." Elsie cocked her head slightly. "What happened?"

"It's a long story. Circumstances kept us apart for years, and we only reunited a couple of months ago."

"Oh my goodness!"

"But we aren't talking about me. This is about you. What are you confused about? Are you in love with him or not?"

Elsie swallowed. "I don't think at this point it matters

much. I did a horrible thing last night and I doubt he'll want anything to do with me."

"Play practice is in half an hour – I'd say he'll have *something* to do with you."

"That's just it! I know I have to face him, but … I'm dreading it. Not because I'm humiliated, though there is that, but …"

"Yes?" Annie prompted.

Elsie looked at her and fought to keep her lower lip from trembling. "Why does it hurt so much? The thought of seeing him, knowing I made such a fool of myself last night?"

"Dare I ask what happened?" Annie asked then took a sip from her cup.

"I kissed him."

Annie choked on her tea.

"I know! It was highly improper! But that wasn't the worst of it! I, I … I kissed him, and then I tried to get Grandpa to, to force him to marry me … more or less."

Annie put a hand to her mouth and closed her eyes. Was she trying *not* to laugh?

"Well?" Elsie said. "Can you see my dilemma?"

Annie giggled. "Oh, Elsie, that's not much of a dilemma. You had a moment of foolishness, yes, but we all do. It's hardly a hanging offense."

"But I can't face him today! I just can't!"

"Why did you kiss him?"

Elsie closed her eyes a moment and took a deep breath. "I felt so overwhelmed yesterday with what happened to Grandma, and when Bowen came in and touched her and she … she …"

Annie's face calmed. "I know, it's sometimes over-whelming to see the Lord at work, but know that what happened with your Grandma yesterday was indeed a miracle."

Tears filled Elsie's eyes. "Grandpa told me last night that she wasn't breathing, then Bowen came in and … and … and that's why I kissed him, because we almost lost her, and I've lost everyone in my life that I've ever loved, and …"

Annie reached across the desk and touched Elsie's hand. "You don't have to be ashamed of anything. You were overwrought and were reaching out. Trust me, I know what that's like. Also, you may very well be in love, and there's nothing wrong with that."

Elsie wiped her eyes. "I'm being such a ninny. But … I don't think Bowen feels the same way."

Annie smiled. "As I said before, I've seen the way he looks at you. My advice is this: don't be afraid to love, Elsie. Don't make the mistake of waiting to make sure the other person loves you first before you give your heart away. It's okay to guard your heart as the Good Book says, especially with a growing love, but don't be stingy with it."

Elsie sat and stared at the teacup in her hands. "So, in other words, face him as if nothing happened?"

"No, face him as if it *all* happened, as a woman who went through a lot yesterday. Besides, there's only a little over two weeks until our play and you're going to be spending a lot of time with Bowen between now and then."

Elsie closed her eyes and sighed. "That's what I'm afraid of."

"Why?"

"Because I'm afraid that by the time we perform the play, I'll be completely and hopelessly in love with Bowen Drake."

Annie got up, went around the desk and hugged her.

"And what's so bad about that?"

"Well, he didn't seem too interested in a shotgun wedding after I kissed him."

Annie laughed again. "Oh, dear! You don't do anything halfway, do you?"

Elsie couldn't help but smile. "Trust me, when I set out to humiliate myself I do a good job. Even Mr. Berg thought so."

"Mr. Berg? What does he have to do with all this?"

"He was at the house at the time. He came downstairs with Grandpa and, er … removed Bowen from my person."

"Oh, my. He didn't hurt him, did he? I noticed neither of them were in church this morning …"

"I don't know what happened to them. Mr. Berg just said he was taking Bowen to the saloon for pie."

"Pie?" Annie went pale.

Elsie looked at her, dumbfounded. "What? What is it?"

"Oh, that explains everything! Including why they weren't in the service this morning. Well … you don't need to be worried one bit. I think Mr. Drake feels more for you than he'd like to admit, especially if *pie* is involved."

"Really? But … what does having a piece of pie have to do with any of it?"

"I guarantee it wasn't just one piece. Or even one pie."

Elsie's brow couldn't furrow any farther. "I don't understand at all …"

Annie smiled and squeezed Elsie's hand. "Well, from what I understand, in most places men will try to drown their sorrows over a woman with whiskey. But here in Clear Creek they do it with pie. Mr. Berg started that tradition, and it's caught on from there."

Elsie rubbed her forehead with one hand. "This is a very strange town. Who ever heard of such a thing?"

"Only in Clear Creek, my dear. Only in Clear Creek."

Twelve

BOWEN SLOWLY WALKED INTO THE church and sank down in the nearest pew. His stomach pained him terribly, but he knew that he needed to show up to play practice or suffer the wrath of Andel Berg – probably in the form of another pie.

How on Earth could anyone put away so many blasted pies? It was unnatural! Either that, or Bowen was a complete sissy when it came to pie-eating. He didn't think he was, even though he barely finished three the previous night. Patrick Mulligan, who joined the contest after Bowen gave up, wolfed down four. But Andel Berg took down six!

Madness! There was no other way to describe the fevered frenzy of the crowd as they cheered on the contestants and, finally, after the table was littered with empty pie tins, congratulated the winner with hoots, whistles, and hat-throwing. Bowen had found himself in need of a hat, too, though for a different kind of hurling. He wasn't sure whose he'd ended up using when he lost more than just the contest, but he'd silently promised the poor fellow a new one. He was sure he'd hear about it sometime today, and thereby would find out to whom the hat belonged. Poor fellow.

Poorer still was Paddy Mulligan – Bowen had heard Irene Dunnigan, who baked for the saloon, and Sally Upton, the hotel cook, give the man a double-barreled tongue-lashing that morning. The noise had woken him up to the pain caused by what he'd done the night before. His poor stomach couldn't handle such foolishness twice. Then and there he resolved to never have more than one slice of pie again!

Unfortunately, by the time he awoke, it was too late to go to church. Mrs. Dunnigan and Mrs. Upton must have caught poor Patrick on his way out to let him have it. The men of Clear Creek would have no Sunday pie to go with their lunch or supper - but from what he remembered last night, they probably didn't mind. The women *did* mind, and were clearly upset.

But enough of all that. He was here now, and that's what mattered. He promised Andel he would not toy with Elsie Waller's feelings, that he would remain a gentleman, that he would do right by the girl or suffer the consequences ... he cringed at the thought. He hoped the consequences would *not* involve copious amounts of baked goods.

But how did he feel about her? The question had plagued him last night – not so much whether he was falling in love with Elsie Waller, but whether he was willing to give up his vendetta against his father and his *alma mater* in order to have her.

He fought off a chill and watched as more people entered the church for rehearsal. Harvey Brown walked to the front and proudly held up his costume for all to see, followed by Sheriff Hughes. The men gathered around and studied each other's costumes, oohing and aahing at Mary Mulligan's handiwork.

Bowen watched in silence, if only to distract himself from thoughts of Elsie, and smiled. The people of Clear Creek were a far cry from Philadelphia high society or the Brahmins of Boston and Cambridge. They were simple folk who worked hard, ate well, and loved unreservedly. It didn't hurt that Clear Creek was home to more than a few good cooks, many of which were beautiful women as well.

And the number of both was growing – for instance, Mr. Van Cleet had brought in the three Upton women to work in the hotel. Two were fantastic cooks, and Cyrus was growing worried that he might lose both to matrimony soon. One was being courted by Jefferson Cooke, stepfather to the famous Cooke brothers. The other, Mary Beth, had just agreed to let Harvey Brown squire her around.

He was wondering what Elsie's cooking was like when he saw her emerge from a side door behind the organ. Instinctively he straightened in the pew and smiled. She was lovely, and he shivered at the sight of her.

Could he stand to lose her after the play was over? Would his luck run out again and leave him to watch her fancy someone else? But … Elsie Waller hadn't kissed someone else. She'd kissed *him*, and made quite a point afterward of saying so. She'd even stood her ground when confronted by her grandfather and Andel. (All right, maybe she'd overdone it with all the talk of a shotgun wedding, but at least it showed she cared!)

The question was, would she feel the same way about him this afternoon?

Annie King had followed Elsie out of the room and onto the platform. She spied Bowen sitting in the back, smiled, turned to Elsie and pointed him out.

Bowen felt his stomach knot up and his jaw tighten. What was he going to say to her? What was she going to say to him? What would everyone else think? What …?

She came toward him slowly, as if approaching a timid animal. When she finally reached the pew she gave him a tentative smile. "Hello, Mr. Drake. I hope you are well?"

Bowen grimaced. He hadn't thought about what *she* might think of his pitiful pie antics. Surely she'd heard about it by now. Well, no hope for it now … "I'm not at my best," he replied, placing a hand on his stomach to illustrate. "But I shall survive. And you?"

She nodded as she nervously twisted a loose thread on her dress. He watched her and waited. Was she embarrassed about last night? He noticed the pink in her cheeks, how she looked at the floor, and the wisps of hair that had come loose from the braid she'd coiled and pinned to the back of her head.

She was so beautiful, and once again he had to fight the urge to take her in his arms and kiss her senseless. Or maybe it would be better if she kissed *him* senseless! Then perhaps he'd stop worrying so much about whether she'd still be a part of his life after the play …

"Are we ready to start?" Annie King asked.

Those already gathered nodded.

"Gentlemen, if you have your costume, go ahead and put it on so we can see how it looks. You can change in Preacher Jo's office – he's waiting there to help you."

Harvey and the other men gave a whoop and headed for the door behind the organ.

"We … should join the others up front," Elsie said shyly.

"Yes," Bowen agreed. Their eyes met and he felt his entire body realign itself as if looking at her made his insides fall into place. Before he'd felt disjointed, not just physically (or gastronomically), but as if his very soul wasn't where it was supposed to be. One look at her, and all his metaphysical discomfort vanished. Odd.

"Bowen …" Elsie swallowed hard. "I'm sorry for the way I acted last night. It was terribly … ah …"

"Wonderful."

She started. "W-w-what did you say?"

He leaned toward her and lowered his voice. "I said it was wonderful."

She leaned back a few inches. "It ... *was*?"

"Oh yes."

She froze, eyes wide – in fear or joy, he couldn't tell which. "Well, I ... I didn't mean to ... uh ... you know ..."

"Kiss me? I was under the impression that you very much meant to."

She looked nervously around. "We shouldn't be speaking of this here!"

"Where would you like to speak of it?"

She again stared at him, now smiling nervously. "You aren't going to make this easy for me, are you?"

He smiled at that. He was suddenly feeling mighty bold at this point. "Should I? I was the one kissed. Aren't you going to make an honest man out of *me* now?"

She pressed her lips together to keep from laughing, not altogether successfully. "I'm so sorry; I had a horrible time of it yesterday with what happened to Grandma. My behavior was abhorrent, unforgivable ...."

"Think what you will, but I thought it was rather nice myself."

"You did? You, you aren't upset? You don't think me a ..."

He stepped out into the aisle and looked into her eyes. "I think what you did was very brave. I understand about yesterday. It's very upsetting to watch someone you love suddenly get sick or hurt and be helpless to do anything about it. Trust me, I know." He stopped himself there, and hoped she didn't ask for details. He didn't like to talk about what happened to his mother, nor his father's neglect of her. His father's pride and hunger for recognition had blinded him to the needs of his own family. And what had it gotten him? Nothing but brokenness, and a pell-mell rush to other father figures who were just as flawed.

"Are you ready?" Annie King asked as she came down the aisle.

Elsie turned to her and smiled. "Yes, we're ready now."

Annie looked at them both and smiled back. "Good. We need to talk about your costumes before we get started. Elsie, have you gone to see Mrs. Mulligan yet?"

"No, I'm afraid I haven't. Should I speak with her this afternoon?"

"That would be wise. You as well, Mr. Drake. Christmas Eve is a little over two weeks away, and she'll need time to get them finished. And if your costumes need adjustments, she'll need time to fix them."

Bowen glanced to the front of the church where Harvey Brown was doing his best to pick up the biblical-like robe he wore and walk. It was at least a half a foot too long for him but he still managed to prance about like a peacock showing it off.

"Elsie, you'll need a head covering too. If we can't pin it to your hair, you might have to get used to holding it in place with one hand during the play."

"Oh. Well, couldn't I use a scarf or something to practice with until Mrs. Mulligan finishes my costume?"

"Good idea – do you have one with you?"

"No, I didn't bring one today."

"Well, bring a scarf, or better yet a small blanket, with you tomorrow. In the meantime, here." Annie untied the lace scarf around her neck.

Bowen stiffened and Elsie gasped as they stared at Annie's neck. It was covered in scars, as if someone had taken a knife to her and cut just enough to make marks, but not to kill. "Oh!" Elsie exclaimed. "How ... er, what happened to ...?"

"We all have scars, dear," Annie said softly. "Mine have made me who I am today."

Tears formed in Elsie's eyes. "I'm so sorry! I can't imagine what it must be like ..."

"To have these? Mine are visible, that's all. They're a reminder of a part of my life that was indeed horrible. But what kind of person would I be without them? My life might have been better, perhaps, but I wouldn't understand the healing love of the Lord or of the people in this town." She smiled again and put a hand on her neck. "One day I'll tell you the story behind these. But right now, we need to practice." She turned, strode up the aisle to the front of the church, and gathered the three wise men together to inspect their costumes.

Elsie turned to Bowen. "What do you think happened to her?"

Bowen watched as the preacher's wife gathered the townsfolk around her like a mother hen her chicks. "I don't know. But what she said made a lot of sense."

"Which part?"

"About her scars, and who she'd be if she didn't have them." Bowen put his hand on the small of Elsie's back to guide her up the aisle. His mind whirred with the woman's wise words. He had scars, too – or perhaps more like gaping wounds. Wounds from his mother's death, his father's neglect, his professors' betrayals, his terrible luck on his journey west ... and most of all, from his own un-forgiveness.

Elsie nearly fainted when Bowen put his large, warm

hand on her back and gently pushed her ahead of him toward the front of the church. Her stomach turned a somersault and she fought to keep her eyes on the platform rather than close them in bliss! How would she ever get through the practice now that she knew he didn't think her a complete wanton?

"All right, is everyone here?" Annie called.

"No, ma'am," Harvey Brown answered. "The Cookes and Mr. Berg ain't here yet."

"That's all right – they'll be coming later to be assigned their parts. In the meantime, let's get started with what we have. Wise men, take your places over there." Annie pointed to the center of the platform. Wilfred Dunnigan, Sheriff Hughes, and Patrick Mulligan went where she indicated. "Harvey, you stand over here," she said, indicating the right side of the platform. "You'll either narrate from that side or the other, depending on what's going on."

"Yes, ma'am!" Harvey said, happy as a lark to be the center of attention. He had the most lines in the play.

"Elsie and Bowen, I want the two of you over here for now." She guided them to stage left.

Elsie put the lace scarf over her head as she and Bowen moved into place. She saw Bowen look at her, and caught his eyes as they flashed. What must she look like to him with the lace over her head? What did he think of her? She blushed as she pictured herself in a wedding dress standing at his side, the two of them facing the platform instead of away from it. Her heart warmed at the thought.

But she was getting ahead of herself. She had to remember what Annie told her: to guard her heart as love grew, but not to be stingy with it either. But how was she to do that? Usually when she saw something she wanted, she went after it wholeheartedly. She wasn't one to back away. Could she keep her heart in check and wait for a sign that Bowen was really interested in her, rather than just being polite? Sure, he was flirting with her, and it thrilled her to the bone. But what if he did that with every girl he met? How was she to know if she was special in his eyes?

She continued to ponder her dilemma as Annie directed the remaining men to their places on and around the platform. When all were in place for the opening scene, Annie stepped back to look at her handiwork. "Okay, let's get started. Harvey, you may begin."

Harvey cleared his throat. "I'm here to tell you the story of the birth of Jesus," he said then looked sheepishly around. All eyes were on him, and Elsie and Bowen watched as he reached up and loosened his collar. "A long time ago, there was a girl named Mary."

Elsie curtsied, then looked at her script to make sure that's what she was supposed to do. Bowen smiled at her as she straightened. "Perfect," he whispered. "You're sure to get applause."

She stifled a giggle. "Stop. Pay attention."

"How can I, with you standing next to me looking like an angel?"

Elsie almost melted. Did he really mean it, or was he just flirting again? She fought to keep her tears at bay. Now was not the time for her to become emotional!

"Look! The virgin will conceive a child and, don't ya know it, give birth to a son!" Harvey read with no little exuberance.

Bowen leaned toward her. "Your next cue is coming up."

"Stop!" she scolded him in a whisper.

"'Where is the newborn king of the Jews?' that

no-good, low-down varmint Herod asked of the wise men." Harvey looked at his script, then to Annie. "Is it proper for me to say 'varmint'?"

Elsie laughed at Harvey's question and quickly put a hand over her mouth. Bowen did the same, only his hand was also over her mouth. "We're good here – don't worry about us," he said.

Harvey ignored them and looked from his script to Annie and back again. Annie eyed the pair, rolled her eyes, then motioned for Harvey to continue.

Elsie pulled Bowen's hand from her mouth. "Stop fooling around! You're going to get us in trouble!"

"Too late."

She looked at him then, *really* looked at him. He had that smoldering look in his eyes again, like on the first day she met him. There was no warm cup of coffee in his hands this time, no bowl of stew she'd fed him to bring it about. No, this was for her and her alone, and she felt her head begin to swim. *Oh no, please, no! I can't faint! Good grief, what will he think of me then?* She stood ramrod-straight to keep from toppling over.

He smiled at her and looked deeply into her eyes. "Are you ready to play the part of my wife, Miss Waller?" he asked.

"You really ought to pay attention to the rehearsal," she whispered through gritted teeth.

"But I am paying attention. I'm paying attention to my wife."

"Wife?"

"You *are* my wife, aren't you?"

"Well, yes, but …"

"Shouldn't I pay attention to my wife?"

Elsie's breathing picked up, her spine a tingle as he bent his face to hers. "Well, I … yes, I suppose so."

"You realize we get to kiss in a few scenes?"

"Oh, dear God …" She'd forgotten about that. The room began to spin.

"Perhaps we should get some practice in before our scene?"

"Mr. Drake! Y-you can't p-p-possibly be serious …" Why was she having trouble breathing?

"Oh, but I am," he said, leaning even closer. "Very serious."

His voice was like velvet. She could lose herself in it if she wasn't careful. Suddenly the tables were turned – she was no longer the one in pursuit. Every feminine cell in her body instinctively knew he was *not* just flirting. It unnerved her to no end. She couldn't think, she couldn't breathe, and she … she…

Oh, drat!

That was her last thought as she fell to the ground like a sack of flour.

Thirteen

BOWEN PULLED ELSIE INTO HIS arms the second she began to fall. Good Lord, what was wrong? Had *he* caused this? Was she sick? Was she going to be all right? Did he need to send for Doc Waller? Oh for Heaven's sake, what did he need Doc Waller for? He was perfectly capable of handling the situation himself! "Elsie?" he asked as he gently patted the side of her face.

Annie and the three wise men rushed over. "What happened?" Annie asked.

"She fainted, but I'm not sure why," Bowen said. "She was fine a moment ago."

"I'll go fetch a cup of cold water," Wilfred offered. He turned and rushed off.

Elsie's eyes flutter open, and she gasped when she realized Bowen was supporting her. "Oh my ..."

"Are you all right?" Bowen asked. There was a sternness in his voice that she hadn't heard before.

"I think so. What happened?" she sighed. His eyes held a deep concern in them, and she began feeling woozy all over again. Bowen held her a little tighter in response, which made her smile.

"I think she may be sick!" Harvey blurted. He quickly backed up a step, as did everyone else who'd gathered round.

Except Annie, who saw the look on her face. "No ... I think she's feeling all right," she said dryly.

"Yes, I'm fine. I ... I guess the last couple of days finally caught up to me," Elsie grabbed one of Bowen's arms in an attempt to stand on her own.

Bowen didn't think, only reacted. He gathered her more firmly against him, led her to the nearest pew and sat her down. He looked into her eyes, but not in the same smoldering way as before. It was more like he was examining her, the way Grandpa would. "What are you looking at?" she asked, her voice coming out in a squeak.

"You. You should lie down. Are you dizzy? Any nausea?"

"No. I was dizzy before, but not now."

"Do you feel sick to your stomach?"

"No, not really."

"What do you mean, not really? Either you do or you don't." Bowen caught the harsh tone in his own voice and grimaced. "I'm sorry, Elsie. But I do need to know."

She put a hand on her midriff and looked at him. "No. My stomach's fine."

Bowen sat back and sighed in relief. Thank God. He'd seen enough sickness along the trail to last him a lifetime, over and above the ordeal with his mother. The thought of Elsie falling ill terrified him. Often folks died in the winter from odd ailments, ones that more often than not started out as nothing, only to turn serious.

For one moment he saw in his mind's eye Elsie's beautiful face flushed with fever, her eyes glazed over, her skin pale – and he, the man with the healing touch, helpless to do anything about it because, fool that he was, he'd asked God to take his gift away! He closed his eyes and shuddered at the irony …

"I'm fine; really I am." Elsie's soft voice pulled him from his thoughts. "Are … are *you* all right?"

"Yes, I am. Just … worried about you."

She turned away as she blushed.

"I've brought the water!" Wilfred said as he nearly tripped on the hem of his costume rushing to where they sat.

"Thank you," Bowen said as he took the cup and offered it to Elsie.

She took it from him, but didn't drink. "Maybe we had better get on with the rehearsal." She was embarrassed enough by her fainting spell as it was.

Bowen stood and helped Elsie up. She took a tentative sip of water before handing the cup back to Wilfred. "I don't know what happened. I'm sorry for interrupting practice."

"Don't worry about it," Annie told her. "I'm just glad you're all right." She turned and went back to her place in front of the platform, motioning for the others to resume their posts.

Bowen looked at the sheepish Elsie, and it was all he could do not to pull her into his arms and kiss her till she *really* fainted! But her swoon still concerned him, and he made a point of keeping an eye on her for the rest of the rehearsal. In fact, he found that he couldn't take his eyes off her!

A week and three rehearsals later, Elsie still hadn't gotten over her embarrassment at swooning into the arms of Bowen Drake. And not just that, but she'd swooned *because* of Bowen Drake! What was she, some silly girl with no control over herself? Oh sure, some women thought swooning in front of a man was romantic. Charlotte Davis from back home even practiced her dives in order to achieve the proper response from a man – specifically, from Clayton Riley. That ended after the first time she actually tried it in front of him; his response had been to dump a bucket of cold water over her head to revive her!

But Bowen hadn't poured cold water on Elsie, and he didn't poke fun at her afterwards as Clayton had done (deservedly, Elsie thought) to Charlotte. No, instead she saw something in his eyes she'd never seen before – worry.

Had she scared him? The thought only made her feel worse. She didn't want to be a cause of anguish for him, or anyone else for that matter. She hadn't mentioned the faint to Grandma or Grandpa, and it had been sheer luck that no one else had. No, she'd keep that to herself for as long as she could. Annie and Preacher Jo had shown some concern after rehearsal that day, but didn't make a fuss over it afterward. The Cooke brothers and Mr. Berg had shown up only afterward, and everyone else was too caught up in their parts to pay any more attention to her. Thank Heaven for that!

Christmas was only a week and a half away, and she had to stop worrying about the past and start preparing for the future – namely, the play! She went over and over her lines to memorize them. She and Bowen practiced in a corner each rehearsal while Preacher Jo and Annie directed the others.

Today, they were to have a full dress rehearsal, as almost everyone had their costumes now. She adored the one Sadie and Belle Cooke had made for her, a plain white robe with a pretty blue head covering that looked wonderful with her eyes. It was simple and lovely.

But she was more excited about finally getting to see Bowen in his costume!

"Are you off to practice, child?" Grandma called from the kitchen as Elsie came down the stairs, costume in hand.

"Yes, Grandma."

"Tell Mrs. Mulligan to come by here after practice, will you? Oh, and give this basket of molasses cookies to Mr. Berg. I hear Mrs. Mulligan done finished his costume today."

Elsie gave her a curious look. What did cookies have to do with Mr. Berg's costume? "I will. Anything else?"

"Nope. Have a good time,"

Elsie noted the weariness in Grandma's voice. "Is everything all right?"

"Yes, child," she said with a sigh. "I'm just tired. Seems I get tired a lot easier now than I used to. Now, it ain't your job to fuss over me – you run along."

After a moment, Elsie nodded, wrapped her shawl around herself and left the house. Once outside, she made a mental note to ask Grandpa what might be going on. Grandma seemed well enough since her so-called fainting spell over a week ago, but Elsie had noticed that she was getting tired all the time these days.

Elsie tried to help around the house as much as she could, even aiding Grandpa on a few of his visits to the farms outside of town. One trip was to the Triple-C Ranch to check on Sadie, who despite her constant morning sickness had still managed to work on Elsie's costume. What a blessing that woman was! Elsie had no doubt she'd make a wonderful mother, and Harrison Cooke would be a great – if perhaps over-protective – father. The poor man flitted about the house like a mother hen, driving Sadie crazy at times, but it was easy to see how much they loved each other.

Elise braced herself against the wind and wondered what it would be like to be so in love.

But you already know.

Elsie stopped in her tracks just before the saloon. "No, I don't already know. How could I?" she said to herself.

Because you love Bowen. You know you do. You just won't admit it because you're afraid.

"That's silly!" Elsie said, then realized she'd done it out loud and rolled her eyes. She was going to have to break this habit of talking to herself, at least when she was out in public! If she didn't, folks might start to think she'd gone 'round the bend.

"Excuse me, ma'am," a voice called from the saloon.

Case in point. Elsie felt herself blush as she turned. A bedraggled-looking fellow with an older boy at his side stood on the boardwalk in front of the saloon. She didn't recognize either of them. "Can I help you, sirs?"

"Do ya have a blacksmith in town? We went to the livery stable but no one's there."

"I believe the blacksmith is at the church getting ready for a rehearsal. If you'll follow me, I can take you there."

"Much obliged, ma'am. Thank ya." He and the boy stepped off the boardwalk and joined her in the street. He tipped his dirty hat to her and grinned. His teeth were yellowed and a bottom front tooth was missing. The boy looked to be around twelve or so, his clothes just as ragged as the man's, and Elsie assumed they were father and son. "We just rode in. Been frightful cold out on the prairie."

Elsie stopped and turned to him. "You mean to tell me the two of you have been camped out on the prairie? In *this* weather?"

"Well, it ain't been that bad this last week. We done held up pretty well, considerin'."

Elsie eyes darted over the two of them, their dirt-covered faces and torn clothing. "You poor things!"

The boy coughed a few times, glanced at his father,

coughed some more.

"Oh my! Well, let's go find the blacksmith, then see about something for that cough. I hear Jefferson Cooke can take care of any sort of problem with horses."

The man grinned and again tipped his hat. "Much obliged." The boy coughed a few more times as they set out again. Elsie hurried her pace to get them to the church as quickly as possible.

Once inside, she looked for Jefferson, found him, and brought him to the father and son straightaway. She watched as the three of them left the church for the livery stable, still shaking her head that they had been camped out in the open for the last week. They were lucky to be alive!

She suddenly recalled her first sight of Bowen, and shuddered. His blue lips, his still form ... what if she found him like that now? What would she do? It had been bad enough when she wasn't in love with him, but now ...

Remember to guard your heart, Elsie; guard your heart!

"Easier said than done," she whispered to herself as she sat in the nearest pew. She looked for Bowen, and saw him stepping out of Preacher Jo's office, which was serving as the dressing room for the play. Once the men were done, the ladies would get to use it to change into their costumes.

And change was exactly what Bowen had done. He was handsome enough as it was, but in his costume he was positively ... well, to say it like one of the Cooke brothers, he looked bloody well *incredible!* Her eyes went wide as he approached her, and she belatedly realized her mouth hung open like an idiot's. She snapped it shut just as he reached her.

"What do you think?" he asked. "Mrs. Mulligan got

the hem length right on the first try!"

She looked him up and down. His robe was simple, the sash the same blue as her head covering. He, too, wore the traditional head covering of Biblical times, only his matched the color of his robe. He looked breathtakingly handsome and it was all Elsie could do to not throw her arms around him.

"Well?" he asked again.

"I love it!" She'd almost blurted out "kiss me!" but caught herself at the last second. She turned from him and looked at the bundled costume in her arms, and hoped he thought she looked as good in hers.

Elsie closed her eyes. Yep, she'd gone and done it. She knew without a shadow of a doubt that she was madly in love with Bowen Drake.

Bowen stood next to Elsie. She was so beautiful, he was having to ball his hands into fists to keep himself in check. When did he get to kiss her? That scene couldn't come fast enough!

"Is everyone ready?" the Rev. King called out. He looked over the townsfolk present and did a quick head-count. "Where's Mr. Berg?"

Duncan Cooke laughed. "He's having a little trouble with his costume. He'll be along."

Preacher Jo smiled, nodded, and left it at that. "All right, in this scene Mary and Joseph have just arrived at the inn. Where are my innkeeper and his wife?"

Two of Mr. Van Cleet's men, who'd been sitting in the back waiting for their scene, hurried to the front of the church. The shorter man was dressed as a woman, not too successfully, and the rest of the townsfolk were having to hold in their laughter. Preacher Jo rolled his eyes and looked to Annie for help, but she was snorting and coughing along with everyone else.

Elsie quickly gave up, and began laughing so hard she had to hang onto Bowen for support. Her touch was like fire, burning right through his costume to the flesh beneath. The urge to take her into his arms was almost too much to bear. He suddenly looked into her eyes and knew he was lost, lost to this woman who had found him half-frozen in the snow mere weeks before.

How could he possibly leave Clear Creek come springtime? Stupid question; he couldn't.

The noise died down as everyone attempted to catch their breath. Bowen and Elsie's eyes were locked now. A roar went up, but neither of them could pull their gaze away to look at what had everyone guffawing this time. They had to rely on their hearing to discern the situation:

"Hey, Berg!" Sheriff Hughes called out. "What in tarnation are you supposed to be?"

"Isn't it obvious?" Andel Berg answered.

"Sure tisn't, laddie," Mr. Mulligan cried. "You look like a bundle o' fresh cornstalks!"

"Or a giant pickle what's spoilt!" Wilfred laughed.

Mr. Berg growled in frustration. "I'm a tree!" he boomed. "How can none of you see that?"

The townsfolk fell into hysterics.

Finally, Elsie and Bowen were able to pull away from each other and turn to view the sight. Elsie doubled over and burst into laughter. "Now I know what the cookies were for!"

Bowen was too stunned to do much more than goggle. Poor Andel Berg looked like a monstrous green plant that had seen better days – and possibly a hurricane or two. "What cookies?" he managed to ask.

"The ones ... in the basket ... over there," Elsie answered while trying to catch her breath. "Grandma told me to ... to give them to Mr. Berg ... I think they're his favorite..."

Bowen tried to shake himself out of his stupor. "Maybe you ought to give them to him before he clobbers the wise men."

Elsie nodded, struggled to her feet and went to retrieve the basket. She made her way through the others and held it up to Mr. Berg.

Bowen watched her, and his heart warmed – not only at the sight of Elsie, but of the townspeople of Clear Creek. They'd grown on him, grown in such a way that he thought he might just be able to let go of his vendettas, to leave it all behind him and start fresh. He *could* make a new life in Clear Creek ... with Elsie at his side ...

He suddenly stiffened. He'd been out on the trail too long not to recognize what it felt like to have someone sneaking up behind you. He turned and scanned the rest of the church but saw nothing. The townsfolk were still heckling Mr. Berg. Elsie was still holding up the basket. The Reverend had his face in his hand and was shaking his head in chagrin. Everything was normal.

So why did he get the distinct feeling he was being watched?

Fourteen

A WEEK LATER ELSIE WAS SITTING in the parlor with Grandma, knitting. She was making Grandpa a scarf and mittens for Christmas, while Grandma put the last touches on a shirt she'd made for him. She snipped off the thread and secured the button she'd just sewn on. "Land sakes, if your Grandpa can't make this shirt last I don't know what I'll do. He wears 'em out quicker than I can put 'em together!"

"How does he wear them out so fast, Grandma? It's not like he's out working in a field all day or doing a lot of manual labor."

"Oh, of course not, child. It's on account of the blood."

Elsie stopped her knitting and looked at her. "Blood?"

"He's a doctor, and sometimes doctoring can get mighty messy. I could scrub those shirts of his 'til kingdom come and never get all the blood out."

"Oh." Elsie said quietly. "I never thought about it before. Is it hard being married to a doctor?"

Grandma thought on it a moment. "No. Leastwise, not when you care about people as much as he does. I guess he and I always were the doctoring sort, mending folks that need it. I've been married to your Grandpa for so long I can't remember when I wasn't working at his side."

"How long have you and Grandpa been married?"

"Oh, a frightful long time!" Grandma laughed. "Let me see … got to be near fifty-five years, I'd say."

Elsie looked at her, wonder in her eyes. To be in love

with someone for fifty-five years, and to love them still … how romantic! "Did he sweep you off your feet, Grandma?"

"Oh, yes! One day I'll tell you about it – but right now I've got to get supper started." She set down her sewing but didn't get up. Instead, she watched Elsie knit for a moment before she spoke. "You ever think about marriage, child? You're old enough now to have it on your mind."

Elsie finished knitting the row she was working on, then set her needles in her lap. "Yes, I've … thought about it."

"Anyone in particular you fancy here in town?" Grandma smiled as if she already knew the answer to her question.

Elsie couldn't help but blush; she knew Grandma knew. "I guess it's kind of obvious…"

"And Bowen Drake fancies you, too. Anyone can see it."

Elsie tried to remain calm. "He does?"

"Oh, come now, child – you may be young, but you ain't dumb! Of course he does! He's a terrible flirt, but he only flirts with you. He watches over you like a guard dog when you're at play practice. And any time he sees you in town, he's instantly at your side. No one else dares come near you. In fact, none of the men from the hotel have come sniffing around here – no cuts, no bruises, nothing broken."

"Maybe that's because Bowen Drake mends them before they have the chance to come," Elsie said, then covered her mouth.

"Oh, I think you're right. Just as well, as Doc's been busy going to the outlying farms these last two weeks treating folks that's ill. Like I said before, there's more to Bowen Drake than meets the eye. He doesn't realize it but he's been a big help to your Grandpa. With all the new folks in town, he and I can't keep up with all the doctoring that needs doing anymore."

"I'm glad Bowen... I mean, Mr. Drake is such a big help."

Grandma chuckled. "You don't have to be calling him 'Mr. Drake' – not after that kiss you laid on him a few weeks ago!"

Elsie's jaw dropped in shock. "I ... I ..."

Grandma laughed out loud and shook her head. "Oh child, when will you learn you can't keep things from me? And I don't see nothing wrong with what you did – except for all those hysterics about a shotgun wedding right after. You know, why don't you invite Bowen to Christmas dinner? He might enjoy a quiet evening with us instead of grubbing with Mr. Van Cleet's men at the hotel."

Elsie was still getting over her shock at finding out Grandma knew of her slip-up – and didn't exactly disapprove. "Well ... I hear Mrs. Upton has quite a feast planned. Mr. Van Cleet's men are very excited about it. They're out looking for a tree for the hotel even now."

"Well, you ask him anyhow. I know he'd love to sample your cooking. All men do before they ..." she stopped short and smiled.

"Before they what, Grandma?"

Grandma grinned ear to ear. "Before they propose."

"Propose?!" Elsie stood, her knitting forgotten. "Oh, Grandma! You don't honestly think Bowen Drake plans on proposing to me, do you?"

"Why wouldn't I? Trust me, child - around here, once a man gets it in his mind to pursue a woman, a proposal ain't far behind. There's too much competition around for anyone to be patient with a lengthy courtship."

Could it be true? Did Bowen Drake feel for her the same Elsie felt for him? She could barely make it through play practice now, he was such a distraction to her — she kept forgetting her lines, missing her cues, standing in the wrong spot. Yesterday she forgot to bring the baby Jesus (actually a log with a baby's face whittled into it by Wilfred and wrapped in a blanket) to rehearsal. He'd given it to her the day before and told her it was for the play. She marveled at the realistic face and how the wood carving, when wrapped in a blanket, really did look like a baby. And then the next morning, she'd left it sitting in the parlor like a dolt. Good thing it wasn't a real baby …

She knew she loved Bowen, but still she fought to keep it to herself, to bury it as best she could. What if he didn't feel the same? Sure, he showed some affection for her, and just as Grandma had said, anyone could see it. Annie King smiled at her whenever Bowen was near, and Mr. Berg looked on approvingly — when he wasn't busy being a tree, that is. In fact, everyone in the play seemed to approve the match; they made no fuss when Bowen took her hand in rehearsal and led her around the stage during scene changes. Even Fannie Fig didn't bother gossiping about it anymore.

Now Christmas Eve, and the play, were only a few days away. Elsie told herself to be careful and wait until after Christmas to let Bowen see how she felt. After all, if he still planned to leave come spring, he'd be thinking about it a lot more once the play was past. There would also be no reason to be with her unless he took it upon himself to come see her - which she would consider a courting gesture. In fact, the whole town would. But until then, she'd guard her heart … or at least try not to make a fool of herself again.

"I'll start supper. But you think about what I said," Grandma said. "Doc and I would love to have Bowen for Christmas dinner, and I know you would too. Besides, it wouldn't be the first time a dinner with a young man in this house sparked a proposal."

"It wouldn't?" Elsie asked as she stooped to pick her knitting up off the floor.

"Of course not, child. What do you think tipped the scales for Harrison Cooke when he first set eyes on Sadie? Nothing like a good home-cooked meal, a wonderful pie and a pretty girl to get thoughts of matrimony swimming in a man's mind. All right, maybe not pie in this case. But wrap it all up with a Christmas tree, and that man's bound to have the words "will you marry me" spilling from his lips in no time!"

Elsie blushed at the thought, and smiled. "I … I hope you're right."

Grandma shook her head as she headed for the kitchen. "Oh child, I *know* I'm right."

Elsie had an extra bounce in her step the next day on her way to play practice. Christmas Eve was only three days away, and she was belatedly thinking of what to give Bowen as a gift. Previously she'd convinced herself it would be improper to do so – he hadn't hinted about giving her one, after all. But why should she deny herself the pleasure? He certainly could use a new scarf and a pair of mittens – especially after his ordeal when he first came to town. She'd have to knit at top speed to get them done in time! But if he was to have Christmas dinner at the Wallers', she could give them to him then. That would give her a little extra time …

She had to fight to keep from skipping into church with the thought. Christmas dinner with Bowen Drake! Grandma was right, she knew it in her heart. If Bowen continued to want to see her after the play, that would confirm it. And a marriage proposal wouldn't be long in following …

A chill went up her spine as she settled into a nearby pew to wait for Bowen to emerge from the dressing room. The men got to the church a good half-hour before the women to change - it was easier for the women to simply wear theirs to play practice at this point, as Elsie had. She removed her coat, hung it over the back of the pew, and replaced her bonnet with the blue head covering.

Just as she sat again, Bowen came out of Preacher Jo's office with the tree, er … Mr. Berg. Elsie fought against giggles at the sight – the poor man really did look ridiculous, at least until he held his arms out. Then, she had to admit, he managed to appear more lifelike… er… tree-like. Preacher Jo had found a part for all who wanted one, and a few who didn't – he'd roped all three Cooke brothers and Mr. Berg into the production. Harrison and Colin were ranchers (in lieu of shepherds), Duncan was the angel Gabriel, and … well, what kind of tree Mr. Berg was, no one knew, but they all found it hilarious. Especially since he was in almost every scene!

"Hello," a familiar deep voice purred.

Elsie thought she might faint again! "Hello," she croaked, her mouth suddenly dry. How was she to get through the next few days if she couldn't keep her heart from leaping out of her chest at the mere sight of Bowen Drake?

He sat next to her in the pew and looked into her eyes. "Are you ready for this? We have only today and tomorrow to practice, you know."

Of course she knew – she'd been counting the *hours* she'd spend with him between now and Christmas! "Oh … why, I hadn't realized. We've been so busy…"

He laughed quietly. "You are a horrible liar, Elsie Waller."

She looked at him, eyes wide, and gasped. The man was intoxicating!

"You know very well how much time we have – you mentioned it only yesterday."

"Oh," Elsie said flatly. "So I did." She'd forgotten about that.

"I don't know about you, but I'm going to miss this," he said as he swept his arm in front of them to indicate the people and the makeshift stable at the front of the church. "I'm going to miss you," he added, his voice soft.

She was thrilled and crushed at the same time. "M-miss me?" she squeaked.

"Yes. I've gotten used to teasing you these last weeks. You know, you're mighty pretty when you're blushing and flustered."

She blushed at that moment; how could she not? She couldn't stand it any longer. "Are you leaving after the play?" she said in a rush as she faced him.

"Leaving? Whatever do you mean?"

Oh no – what a stupid thing to say! Elsie could feel the hot sting of tears at the back of her eyes and a dull ache in her throat. Her heart dropped into her belly like a bucket of rocks. All she could manage in that moment was a pitiful whisper. "I was … were you going to leave Clear Creek after the play? You'll have no reason to stay …"

"Why, Miss Waller, if I didn't know any better I'd say you were trying to get rid of me!" He scooted a few inches closer. "Are you?"

She swallowed. Why did she always become so emotional, so irrational where he was concerned? "No, no, no, of course not!"

"Then what's wrong, Elsie? You look like you're about to spout water."

Was it *that* obvious? "How silly is that? Why would I cry over ... over ..."

"Over my leaving?"

She looked up at him. "Oh, Bowen ..." The first tear fell.

He put one arm over the back of the pew. "Elsie Waller, I don't plan on leaving town ... unless you tell me to."

Her heart leaped from the pit of her stomach and headed for the moon! It was true – he did care for her! She looked up at him and saw it in his eyes. "Oh, Bowen!"

He smiled and lowered his head to hers.

Suddenly they realized they were no longer alone in the back of the church, and glanced up. The three wise-acres stood in the pew in front of them, blocking their view of the others.

"Ain't ya gonna kiss her?" Wilfred Dunnigan whispered out of the blue.

"What is it with you and kissing, lad?" Patrick Mulligan hissed. "You're *always* asking the younguns if they're gonna kiss! You're acting like an old maid!"

"Well, it's obvious he wants to!" Wilfred shot back in a hushed voice. He again looked at Bowen and Elsie. "Go ahead if ya wanna! Ain't no one gonna see ya while we're standing here blocking the view!"

Elsie felt herself turn a furious shade of red.

"You could tell everyone you were practicing," Sheriff Hughes suggested.

Elsie fought for composure. "I can't believe you three are suggesting that–"

She never got to finish. "Turn around," Bowen ordered

the men, making a circling motion with his finger.

"What?" Wilfred squawked as quietly as he could.

"You heard the man," Patrick scolded Wilfred. "Show some respect, laddie!" Reluctantly the three men turned, facing the other way but still blocking everyone else's view of the couple.

"That's better," Bowen whispered. Then before Elsie could react, he snatched her into his arms and kissed her soundly on the mouth. But when he pulled away, there was a distinct sound of what could *only* be a kiss. It drew the attention of Andel Berg, who immediately began stalking down the aisle toward them.

But any menace he posed was quickly headed off by the raised hand of Sheriff Hughes. "I understand you're just being protective, Andel – but leave 'em be this time."

Andel stopped his charge. His brow furrowed as if to say, *are you sure about this?*

"Stand down, son," Wilfred concurred. "Or you'll never eat another pie in this town again."

That got the big man's attention. Slowly he unclenched his branches, took a deep breath and finally said calmly, "Mr. Drake, Miss Waller? It's time for your scene." Without another word, he headed back to the stage.

Elsie suddenly realized Bowen's arms were still around her. Blushing once more, she eased out of his embrace and stood with as much dignity as she could muster. Only then did the wise men disperse.

Bowen also stood and walked with Elsie to the stage. When they arrived, Andel caught him by the arm. "I trust you've had sufficient time to rehearse the next scene?" he asked. The giant's voice was calm, but there was mortal threat in the undertones.

Bowen made sure not to smile, instead glaring up at Mr. Berg. Meet force with force. "I believe so. But if you think we should take a moment longer to prepare ourselves, I'm more than happy to comply."

Elsie flushed red. So did Andel. But he didn't let go of Bowen's arm, not yet. "Remember what we spoke of."

Bowen put a hand on the other man's shoulder and gave it a healthy squeeze. "How could I forget? And again, thank you."

Mr. Berg smiled, released him and went to his spot on the stage.

"What was that about?" Elsie asked.

"You'll see. But right now, it's our turn. And you know what?"

"What?"

Bowen leaned down to her and whispered. "This is the scene where I get to kiss you."

Elsie found she couldn't keep the grin off her face. And for once, she didn't care.

Christmas Eve dawned clear, bright and cold. Bowen spent a good part of the morning in Dunnigan's Mercantile, looking for just the right Christmas gift for Elsie. He was surprised when Mrs. Dunnigan offered to help, and even more so by her ideas for a gift. He finally settled on a silver-plated mirror, comb and brush set, along with a beautiful necklace. It took a good portion of his pay, but he didn't care. He'd been planning on saving for a better horse come spring, but that could wait if he wasn't going anywhere.

He'd decided it right after the wise-men-aided kiss three days before: he was going to stay in Clear Creek, court Elsie Waller, and come springtime make an honest woman of her! That is, if he could wait that long! That kiss, and the ones that had followed during practice that day, were all he'd thought about for hours afterwards.

Besides, Andel had helped him realize that sometimes a man is called to do something with his life that he didn't expect, or even seek. The giant ought to know – he'd been captain of the royal guard in a far land, came to America as a spy on the trail of the Countess Van Zuyen and her daughter Madeline, and disguised himself as a humble blacksmith to infiltrate the town and get closer to his quarry. His job had been to retrieve Maddie – actually, *Princess Madeleina* – and return her to her country. He'd done the first part, and would see to the second part in the spring. What he hadn't counted on, as he explained to Bowen, was marrying her and becoming the future king of the very same foreign country he'd served! Or would it be prince consort? He still wasn't sure, but he also wasn't worried about it.

Who would have thought such things could happen? But in Clear Creek, they did. And who would have thought Bowen Drake could finally let go of all that anger and abandon his plans for revenge? If someone had told him that a simple slip of a country girl would do the trick, he never would've believed it! But he believed it now.

He smiled as he made his way to the livery stable to check on his horse. He was trying to fatten him up during the winter months and make a decent animal out of him before he sold him and got himself a better one. He'd have to find some kind of work after the hotel was finished, and would definitely need a good steed if he got hired on at the Triple-C. Mr. Berg said he'd talk with the Cooke brothers about it.

"Hello?" Bowen called out as he entered. Jefferson Cooke had been the acting blacksmith since Mr. Berg got married, but he was getting on in years and lately hadn't been around much. It wasn't just his age that kept him out of the drafty stable, though – he usually ate his meals at the hotel, the better to spend time with the Upton sister he fancied.

Bowen went to his horse's stall and took in the sight of the sorry animal. "You need to bring me a good price come spring, boy," he said as the horse stuck its nose over the stall door for a pat.

"And *yew* need to do *me* a big favor if ya want that little gal of yours to stay alive," came a gruff voice from behind.

Bowen spun around just in time for his head to connect with the end of a shovel. It stunned him long enough for the man wielding it to punch him square in the gut.

Bowen sank to his knees, the breath knocked from his lungs, and looked up. "You?" he rasped in surprise.

"Yep!" his assailant laughed. "Ya miss me?" But he didn't give Bowen time to answer. He once again smacked him with the shovel and sent him to the cold, hay-strewn ground of the stable. Then he bent over the unconscious form, grabbed him and dragged him into the shadows.

Fifteen

"BOWEN DRAKE. 'S BEEN A long time …"

Bowen opened his eyes slowly. His head hurt tremendously and his vision was blurred. He instinctively tried to swing at the man bent over him, and discovered that his hands were bound behind his back. He tried to curse, but it was muffled. He'd been trussed up, gagged, and propped against the wall of a stall in the livery stable.

"Oh, I know what yer thinkin'. Yer thinkin' that any moment the blacksmith or someone else is gonna come through those doors and find ya here." The man laughed, a sound like a rasp grinding against an iron bar. "Not happenin'. It's Christmas Eve, son. An' ain't no one gonna come tend yer horse – the only horse in this here stable, I might add – when they know ya take care of it ever' day."

Bowen's eyes narrowed.

"Now I'm gonna let ya go just as soon as ya hear me out. First of all … ya do remember me, don'tcha?"

Blurred vision or not, he recognized him. "Of course. How could I forget?" he mumbled around the gag, contempt in his voice.

"Course ya do," the man drawled. "An' yew remember that stage robbery a year or so back, the one where ya got us all arrested. Arrested and sent to rot in that stinking, dank, dark hole of a prison? Ya know most of us died in there? Including my brother … yew remember my brother, don't ya, Bowen?"

Bowen wanted to spit at him, but the gag prevented it.

"My brother had a boy … Little Pete, we called him. 'Cause of you, Little Pete ain't got no pa. So here's how yer gonna make it up to him."

Bowen glared up at the man as memories flashed through his mind. The stage robbery had been written up in several newspapers, both local and beyond. It was one of his father's favorites, he recalled. He'd heard about it from a fellow Harvard alumnus he'd kept in contact with during his outlaw days, who also told him that his old profs were passing the story around as well …

"Yer gonna help us rob the bank while the good people of this town are havin' their Christmas Eve cellybration. Santa Claus, he's gonna make a withdrawal, ya see. An' you're gonna act as his little helper."

Bowen tried to grit his teeth against the gag. His head, and his heart, hurt.

"An' don't yew forget, I got the upper hand here." The man got right in Bowen's face. "'Cause if you don't do 'zactly what I say, Little Pete's gonna kill a few folks, startin' with that purty little gal you fancy. What's her name again – Elsie?"

Bowen lunged at him, but fell right onto his own back.

The man laughed again, then abruptly stopped and glared down at Bowen, resting a boot on his chest for good measure. "Now listen up, Drake, and listen good. Here's what yer gonna do …"

Elsie peeked through Preacher Jo's office door at the townsfolk who were filing into the church and gave an excited little clap of her hands. This was going to be fun!

The church looked lovely. Candles burned here and

there around the stage, and the gas lamps would be turned down during the performance. The men in the audience chattered like hens as they settled into the pews and looked over the sets they'd helped build. There was the door of the inn next to the stable on one side of the stage. On the other was a wall that looked like a house. Her scene with Duncan Cooke, playing the angel Gabriel, would take place there. In the center of the stage was a chair they'd made to look like a throne. Mr. Van Cleet, as Herod, would give his heinous orders from it. They'd also use center stage for the shepherds' – scratch that, *ranchers'* – scene around the campfire, with Duncan standing on the chair to tell the cowhands about the birth of the Savior. And all throughout the play, Mr. Berg was a constant backdrop, a very well-traveled tree. He even had a few lines!

"Miss Waller? Can you help me?" Harvey Brown asked.

She turned, and he pointed to the hem of his robe that was starting to come undone. "Oh my – we're going to have to fix that!" She looked around the office for the sewing kit Mrs. Mulligan had brought for just such an emergency.

Some of the other players milled about in the office, while the rest were helping Mrs. Dunnigan set up the refreshment table at the back of the church. Occasionally Elsie heard the riotous laughter of men teasing the Cooke brothers about their costumes. Duncan was just behind her, his wife Cozette pinning his huge chicken-wire-and-old-bedsheet wings on and adding a few white goose feathers in here and there. It gave him a rather rumpled look, like an angel who'd just finished battling the forces of darkness.

Cozette patted Duncan's shoulder to let him know she

was done. He turned to his wife, kissed her, then edged his way to the back of the room. Not everyone was able to fit in the small office – half the cast had to wait outside behind the sets. Including Elsie and Bowen; their spot was behind and to the left of the stage.

But where *was* Bowen?

Elsie craned her neck to see what was going on at the back of the church. Mrs. Dunnigan stood guard over her arsenal of goodies and her punch bowl, trusty ladle at the ready to dissuade anyone foolish enough to sneak a treat before it was time. The Cookes were heading to their places, though Harrison made a detour to check on his wife Sadie in a pew near the back. Willie the stagecoach driver was looking around for a seat. But no Bowen in sight.

Preacher Jo stepped up to the pulpit and signaled for the audience to quiet down. "Welcome!" he called out. "Merry Christmas, Clear Creek!"

"Merry Christmas, Preacher Jo!" the entire audience called back in unison.

Preacher Jo stood in shock for a second before he smiled. "You didn't practice that, did you?" he teased, knowing full well they must have.

Sure enough, everyone in the audience burst into laughter.

Elsie wasn't laughing. She turned to Annie. "Where's Bowen?" she whispered urgently. "It's almost time for us to take our places."

Annie glanced around. "Good heavens, I don't know! Come to think of it, I haven't seen him at all today!"

"Oh dear!" Elsie said as she again looked toward the back of the church.

"Maybe he's having trouble with his costume," Annie suggested. "Everyone was supposed to wear their costume to church tonight. Josiah still has to read from the Bible and say a few things. You have just enough time to run to the hotel and see if he's there. Mr. Berg?" Mr. Berg carefully made his way to where Elsie and Annie stood. "Have you seen Mr. Drake?"

"No … is something wrong?"

"Well, he's not here yet. He might have gone looking for Mrs. Mulligan at the saloon for help with his costume, but her sewing kit is here. I'm not sure where she is."

"She and Patrick ought to be along," Harvey said. "I know they were still at the saloon when I got here."

"Oh dear, this is terrible! Everyone knew to be here on time! Okay, some of you men escort Miss Waller to fetch Bowen, and take the sewing kit with you. Mr. Berg, might we use your wagon? It'll be quicker to go back and forth that way."

"Certainly."

"I'll let Josiah know to stall. We'll sing some carols to give you more time. Now go fetch him and hurry back."

Elsie nodded, grabbed her coat and the sewing kit, then waited for Mr. Berg to lead the way to his wagon.

"I say, what's going on?" Harrison asked as he came to the office just as they were leaving.

"Bowen's not here," Elsie explained as she put on her coat. "There must be something wrong with his costume."

"I dare say, the chap knew to be here on time!" Colin chimed in. "Best we go find him then."

She followed the two Cooke brothers and Mr. Berg out the side door of the church and into the cold winter night.

Bowen ignored the audible *click* of the gun held to his head. Little Pete wasn't as little as he'd imagined – short, yes, but not young. He had to be in his late twenties, and definitely had a mind of his own. Off the top of his head he couldn't recall the scientific name for the phenomenon, but he'd studied it at Harvard – that unusually slow aging of the body. Then again, who could remember such things with a pistol to their head and a knife poking them in the back?

At least both of them were with him in the bank, not threatening the church full of innocent townsfolk, including Elsie. If he could keep them here long enough, someone was bound to come looking for him. After all, the play was about to start.

"Hurry up, Drake! Ain't got all day!" Harry Deets growled. He'd given Bowen his instructions, then made him wait in the livery stable until sunset. They'd gotten reacquainted while Little Pete went around town with instructions to start shooting townsfolk if Bowen so much as sneezed too loud.

But sneezing was the least of Bowen's worries as they waited. It was frightfully cold outside, and he was becoming more agitated by the minute the longer they sat in the stall. Elsie would no doubt be walking to the church soon, and he wanted to make sure she got there safe and sound. She'd already had one run-in with the outlaws without even knowing it, and he didn't relish her having another. They'd posed as a father and son, conning their way across the Oregon Territory to survive. But when they arrived in Clear Creek in the hopes of a few meals and some fresh horses, they saw Bowen, watched his interactions with the townsfolk, and decided to go for a bigger payload: the bank.

"Can't you open that thing any faster?" Harry said as

he jabbed him with his knife.

"Not when you keep poking at me," Bowen hissed in annoyance.

"Maybe I can find something to make you hurry!" Little Pete squeaked. "That gal of yours is sure pretty; I'd bet if I made her squeal you'd hurry it up!"

Bowen froze with one hand on the safe's combination dial. "You lay a finger on her, you even look at her wrong, and I'll stop altogether," he threatened. Elsie was their hold on him, but he'd figured out he had a hold on them, too – there was no way they could pull this off without his help.

"Nobody ain't gonna get nothin' if yew two don't shut up!" Harry spat. "Now stop it, both of ya! And Drake, yew hurry it up, or pokin'll be the least of yer worries!"

Bowen seethed. If they so much as touched a hair on Elsie's head, he'd do more than stop fiddling with the safe – he'd kill them both. And where *was* everyone? He thought for sure someone would have come looking for him by now!

"I don't understand," Elsie said. "He's not here?" They had searched the hotel and Bowen was nowhere to be found.

"Well, this is a fine mess!" Colin sighed. "The play can't start without Joseph and Mary – you two are in the first scene!"

"Let's check the saloon," Mr. Berg suggested as he pulled up his costume so he could walk better. The four of them left and walked toward the saloon, leaving the wagon in front of the hotel. Music drifted to the edge of town from the church – the singing of the Christmas carols had started.

"We've got to hurry!" Harrison said as he picked up the pace. Mr. Berg easily passed them all with his long legs and went straight for the saloon. Elsie had to run to keep up, Colin keeping a hand at her elbow in case she stumbled in the dark. Once at the saloon they each searched, calling out Bowen's name. But there was no answer.

"Where could he be?" Elsie said to herself. Then a thought struck her: what if Doc hadn't come back from his rounds and Bowen had gone to escort Grandma to the church? "Of course!" she said, hurrying out the saloon doors and onto the boardwalk. She went out into the street and looked toward her house.

Nothing.

No, something. A dim light was coming from inside one of the buildings, one where she hadn't noticed any lights a few minutes before – the bank. But why on Earth would there be a light on in the bank? Was Bowen with Mr. Van Cleet, then?

Throwing caution to the freezing wind, Elsie hurried toward the light. If Bowen was inside with Mr. Van Cleet, there wasn't a moment to lose. There were only so many Christmas carols in the hymnals for the townsfolk to sing! She didn't think to wait for the others – besides, they could easily see where she was going in a town this small.

She ran up the steps and across the boardwalk to the bank, heading straight for the front door. She raised her hand as if to knock, then thought better of it. If Bowen was inside with Mr. Van Cleet, she doubted they'd mind if she just went in. And since they were holding up the play, she figured she had every right …

Then she opened the unlocked door and got the shock

of her life. "Bowen?!"

Bowen froze. "Dear God, no …," he groaned under his breath. Harry had left his side as soon as he'd heard someone run up the steps outside. Whoever it was had a good chance of getting the knife from him and subduing him should he attack. But Bowen hadn't figured on Elsie bursting in, alone and unarmed.

Harry grabbed her from behind as soon as she called out Bowen's name. She started to scream but it was cut off by one of Harry's hands clamping over her mouth, his knife now at her neck. "Well, now! How handy is this?" he chortled as he kicked the door closed with his foot. "What kind of a town is this anyway, Drake? The front door to the bank wasn't even locked? What we break in through the back window for if the front door was unlocked?"

"Let her go," Bowen said, his voice low and menacing.

"Shut up and open the safe, Drake." Elsie's eyes widened over Harry's hand.

Bowen knew what she must be thinking and his gut twisted with the thought. "Elsie …"

"Shut up and open it, or I'll kill her where she stands," Harry warned.

"Let her go or I won't do anything for you. And if you harm her, I will kill you." And Bowen meant it – healing hands or no healing hands, if they hurt Elsie, he would make sure they died even if he had to hunt them down for decades. He noticed Elsie's eyes dart toward the front window. Of course – she must have seen the light of the lantern they were using and come to investigate.

"A standoff, huh?" Harry asked mockingly, and gripped Elsie tighter. He spotted her costume beneath her coat, and the head covering. "Who yew supposed to be, darlin' – the Virgin Mary?"

"You won't get to spend the money if you're dead, Harry." Bowen wanted the outlaw focused on him, not Elsie.

"You ain't gonna marry the gal if'n yer both dead," Harry retorted. "Pete! Keep that gun on him, you idiot! You can have the girl when we're done!"

Little Pete had taken an interest in Elsie, but Harry's order brought his focus back. He shoved the gun into Bowen's cheek. "You heard him; get this thing open so I can have myself some fun!"

"I told you – you touch her and I'll stop." But Bowen knew he was bluffing, even if they didn't – he was out-numbered and outgunned. His mind raced, trying to find a solution beyond just stalling for time. He prayed that Elsie hadn't come searching for him on her own.

Then he spotted an enormous, odd-looking tree out the window, and a flash of white. Sure enough, she hadn't.

He made sure Elsie wasn't so frightened that she'd do something rash, then turned slowly back to the safe to hide a smirk. He hoped that Andel and whoever else was out there knew that Harry had Elsie or she could get hurt.

"Shhh!" Harry suddenly said. "You hear that?"

Little Pete looked at him. "Hear what? I don't hear nothin'."

"And now you're hearing things, Harry?" Bowen said mockingly. "Next you'll be telling us you're worried about the Ghost of Christmas Past." *Keep stalling,* he told himself, *keep distracting them. Buy Andel – and Elsie – all the time you can.* It might not be much, but it was all he could do.

"Shut up, Drake!" Harry hissed as he spun to the window, Elsie still locked in a death grip, the knife at her throat. "Pete, did you hear that scratching sound?"

Bowen almost lunged at the desperado as he turned his back, but thought better of it when he heard a sound come from the back of the bank.

"I heard *that*!" Little Pete said, his brow furrowed in worry.

"Great! Now what do we do?" Harry hissed.

"Give up," Bowen suggested. "Let her go. I can make sure you get out of this alive—"

"SHUT UP, I SAID!" Harry roared, now thoroughly rattled. "We've wasted too much time already! If we cain't have what's in the safe because *someone* won't open it, then we cut our losses and take what we can."

Bowen's eyes narrowed. "Don't even think about it, Harry."

"We ain't leavin' here empty-handed, Drake." Harry's smile was evil. "She'll keep us nice an' warm on the trail, and I fancy myself some decent cookin'."

"You do, you sign your own death warrant," Bowen growled back.

Little Pete laughed as he eyed Elsie with lustful intent. "Sounds like yer writin' checks with yer mouf that yer fists cain't cash—"

With lightning speed, Bowen delivered a textbook uppercut to Little Pete's jaw, knocking him flat on the floor. The gun went flying into the darkness.

Harry, wide-eyed, pressed the knife into Elsie's tender skin as he backed toward the door. But his hands were shaking. "Stay away, Drake, or, or, or I slit her throat!"

"Are you worried I'll cash another check?" Bowen said calmly as Harry continued to drag Elsie to the door. What he could see, and Harry couldn't, was that the door was now wide open. Well, not exactly wide open – it was blocked by over seven feet of angry fake tree.

Harry backed right into the waiting trunk of Andel Berg. He spun around just as a branch – Andel's right arm – descended toward Harry's head. One huge green fist caught him right in the skull as another branch pulled the knife away from Elsie's throat.

Bowen, seeing the knife safely in Andel's hand, lunged at Harry, caught him around the middle, and slammed him onto the floor face-first.

Elsie spun away, and got to watch Bowen pin her captor down and bang his skull on the floorboards twice more to make sure he was out cold. Then he jumped to his feet and ran to her. "Elsie!" he cried, pulling her into his arms. "Elsie, are you hurt? Say something!"

She looked at him numbly. "You … you … you …"

"Yes, sweetheart? What is it?"

"You need to put your costume on," she finished dizzily.

Bowen blinked several times before he realized she was talking about the Christmas play. "Costume … oh, yes. Right."

She looked around the room. "What were you doing? Were you … robbing the bank?"

He didn't have a chance to answer, as Sheriff Hughes, Duncan and Harrison came running in. "What in tarnation is going on here?" the sheriff demanded. "Good grief, who are these fellas? And what were you doing here, Bowen?"

"It's … rather a long story," Bowen replied.

"You'd better start telling it quick, son," Sheriff Hughes remarked. "Those two knew your name, and you knew theirs – I heard that from outside. Who are they?"

Bowen swallowed hard. The moment of reckoning was at hand. "Old acquaintances of mine."

"Acquaintances?" Sheriff Hughes said as he bent over

Little Pete. "Seems to me you oughta watch the company you keep."

"Bowen?" Elsie said, tears in her eyes. "I saw you trying to ... to unlock the safe."

Sheriff Hughes looked at him. "Is that true?"

"Yes and no. I know, I know," Bowen said, holding up a hand, "that's not really an explanation ..."

Duncan bent over Harry, who was just coming around. "You're correct, Mr. Drake. It isn't."

Sheriff Hughes nodded. "And until I get a full explanation, son, I'm afraid you're under arrest."

Sixteen

BOWEN CLOSED HIS EYES, SIGHED and nodded. "I understand, Sheriff." He let go of Elsie and held out his arms as if preparing to be handcuffed.

"No!" Elsie yelled. She stepped between Bowen and the sheriff, pushing Bowen's hands down as she did. "Please, let him talk – I'm sure there's a good reason for all of this!" She stopped, then looked back at Bowen with fear in her eyes. "There … there is a good reason, isn't there?"

Harry Deets came to and saw Duncan standing above him dressed as an angel. He let out a whoop of joy. "I made it! I actually made it!"

Without hesitation, Duncan punched him in the jaw, sending him straight back to the floor. "Start talking, Mr. Drake," he said angrily.

"Look, I wasn't robbing the safe!" Bowen said. "I was playing for time! Those two were holding me against my will!" He looked around for Little Pete's gun, but couldn't spot it.

"But I saw you trying to open it," Elsie replied. "And you were calling them by name."

He quickly turned to her. "And trying to protect *you*. I'm no thief, Elsie. I thought you knew me better than that."

Her face fell at his words. "I thought I did too!" she sobbed. She spun on her heel and headed for the door.

Andel grabbed her arm before she could leave. "Stay,

Miss Waller. Hear him out."

Bowen gave the giant a barely perceptible nod of thanks.

"The play ..." Elsie whimpered.

"The play can wait. This can't." Bowen looked at the sheriff. He might as well get this over with. "Yes, it's true I know these men. I met them over a year ago. I'd ..." He looked down at the floor in shame. "I'd fallen in with some outlaws, and ..."

"You *what*?" Sheriff Hughes asked as he stepped over a still-unconscious Little Pete to get to Bowen.

"You heard me, Sheriff. I rode with these men, and some others. We ... we tried to rob a stage one day ..."

"That ... that makes you an accomplice," Elsie said, her brow furrowing in grief.

"We didn't succeed. I panicked, cut in front of the stage. The driver lost control of the horses and ... well, of all things, they stopped on their own. The men I rode with didn't expect that and figured there must be armed men on the stage, so they scattered, and the driver started trying to pick them off ... in the end no one got hurt. But a posse happened to be heading back to the same town the stage had come from. They rounded them all up, arrested them, and sent them off to jail."

"Why didn't they arrest you?" Duncan asked.

Bowen shook his head and almost laughed. "Because I was credited with saving everyone. If I hadn't cut in front of the stage, there might have been a different outcome." He made a grim face. "I'm not proud of what I did, riding with men like these. I was a fool, and a jackass, and easily the least successful outlaw in the history of outlawry. And then I came here ... half-dead and on the run, and you took me in, and gave me hope, and ... and helped me forgive so many, many things. You showed me I didn't have to rebel, to run away …"

He took a deep breath before continuing. "And then a few days ago, these men came to town, recognized me, and said that if I didn't help them rob the bank, they were going to start killing people."

"What?" Cyrus Van Cleet yelped as he entered the bank. "Is that what's going on? Great jumping horny toads, are you kidding me?"

Bowen sighed. "I wish I was. They threatened Miss Waller most of all."

Elsie's head shot up at that and she stared at him, tears in her eyes.

"Miss Waller?" Cyrus asked. "Why?"

Bowen looked straight at her, closed the distance between them and put his hands on her shoulders. "Because they saw how much I cared for her."

Elsie closed her eyes at his words. "Oh, Bowen; I'm so sorry. So sorry."

He nodded, then removed his hands. "So am I." And, with that, Bowen Drake walked away.

Or tried to. Just as he reached the door, two large hands closed on his right arm and the back of his collar. The first belonged to Andel Berg, the second to Duncan Cooke.

"It may be easier to walk away from a broken trust than to take the time to mend it," Andel stated. "But easier does not mean better."

"What is that supposed to mean?" Cyrus asked.

"He thought he had earned our trust, Mr. Van Cleet," explained Duncan. "Now he feels he's lost it."

"Bowen! You can't leave!" Elsie pleaded.

"But perhaps I should," Bowen replied hoarsely.

"Sheriff Hughes, I think you should place that man under arrest," Duncan said, with a smile and a wink to

Elsie.

"What for? He just explained the whole thing. He saved a lot of folks from getting themselves shot is how I see it, and saved Miss Elsie's life even beyond that. I don't know about you, but I'm feeling pretty foolish right now."

"You'll feel a lot more foolish when my men at the church come to fetch all of you! The play can't start without you!" Mr. Van Cleet cried. "That's why I came over here. Now come on!"

"But what about these two?" Elsie asked as she indicated the unconscious forms on the floor.

"We lock 'em up and get back to the church." Sheriff Hughes explained. "I'm sorry you had such an ordeal, ma'am. Are you sure you're okay?"

"Yes, I'll be fine. I still can't believe they came and tried to rob the bank."

"Bank? What bank?" Mr. Van Cleet asked, his eyebrows raised in question.

"This bank," she said as she waved her hand around the room.

Mr. Van Cleet burst into laughter. "Miss Waller! It's not a bank until it's got money in it!"

"What?" she asked in shock.

"There's no money in the safe yet. They can try to break into it, but it's plumb empty! Would have been fun to see the looks on their faces, though!"

"There … isn't any money here?"

"No, it's in the safe over at the hotel," Bowen explained, turning back around as Andel and Duncan released him. He still sounded unsteady. "Mr. Van Cleet bought this safe for when the bank opens – in March."

"Then … then you weren't robbing the safe, even to help them? You really were stalling!"

"I really was … though I haven't exactly given you

reason to believe mmmph!" The rest was cut off when Elsie ran over, grabbed him by the ears, and kissed him silent.

"Well then," Sheriff Hughes said after a few moments, when Bowen and Elsie still hadn't come up for air. "We'd best lock those outlaws up, then hightail it back to the church. Everyone's waiting on us!"

Fifteen minutes later, after a hasty (and by necessity incomplete) explanation by Preacher Jo to the congregation, Elsie and Bowen were in place, and in costume, for the first scene. "I'm sorry," Bowen whispered.

"You have nothing to be sorry for, Bowen," Elsie said, choking back a sob. "I'm the one who should apologize – for not trusting you."

"I wasn't acting trustworthy. If I'd never fallen in with those outlaws –"

"– then you'd never have saved those people on the stage. And you'd never have come here to Clear Creek, and we'd never have met, and …" Elsie looked him right in the eye. "… and I wouldn't have fallen in love with you."

Bowen's eyes widened. "Or I with you." He paused as his words, as her words, sunk in. "But my past …"

It's just like Annie said. Our past, our scars … they're what make us who we are today. And I like who you are today, Bowen Drake. The least successful outlaw in the history of outlawing," she finished with a smile.

Bowen couldn't speak. Not with words, anyway. But his lips on hers spoke volumes.

Suddenly they heard Harvey Brown's opening line, the applause of the congregation, and they quickly knelt as the play got underway. They said their own lines as they'd practiced them – a little stiffer perhaps, but behind them were three words they spoke to each other over and over: *I forgive you.*

The audience roared with laughter as Andel Berg took the stage, oohed and aahed as Duncan Cooke's angel appeared. Twice she almost broke into tears of joy, but didn't. Twice he almost laughed like a loon, but caught himself. The show must go on.

And when it came time for the scene with the kiss, they were ready. Elsie knelt in front of the makeshift manger with the wooden baby wrapped in a swaddling cloth. She cradled the bundle and looked down at the beautifully carved face of Jesus. She felt Bowen's finger under her chin, pulling her face up to look at his. The three wise men softly hummed "Silent Night" while Harvey spoke his lines.

She looked into his eyes and stifled a sob. *Thank you, God,* she thought, *for bringing us through all this, even if it's just for this one moment.*

He slowly looked down at the baby in her arms, then back to her. He reached out with his other hand and stroked the cheek of the wooden Jesus with a tenderness she never would have believed – as if it was a real child, their child. Then he leaned toward her, his hand still cupping her face, and tenderly kissed her.

The audience was dumbstruck. No roar of applause, no hooting and hollering that he'd kissed her in public. No, they were as awed by the scene as she was.

And Elsie Waller felt in that one kiss something she didn't know one could feel in a kiss at all. Not just the forgiveness of man, but the forgiveness of God. Not just the love of a man, but the love of God through him.

Bowen pulled away and looked deeply into her eyes.

"I'll only leave town, Elsie Waller, if you tell me to. Say so, and I'll ride off tonight and never return. Tell me to stay and, well … you'll never be rid of me."

The entire church went silent. Harvey Brown's jaw had dropped at Bowen's words, words not found in any part of the script. He looked at Annie King in the front pew, who could only shrug in answer. She'd heard what Bowen said, as did the rest of the church, and she waited for Elsie's answer along with everyone else.

Elsie looked up at him, her tears now flowing. "I love you, Bowen Drake."

He smiled. "Then tell me to stay."

She was about to speak when a man in the front pew, one of Mr. Van Cleet's carpenters, blew his nose. She glanced at him and saw the man was crying.

He waved his handkerchief at her. "Well, don't just sit there a-gawking at me, missy! Tell him!"

"Yeah," another man called from a few pews back, also with a handkerchief in his hand. "Tell him to stay!"

Elsie turned back to Bowen, fresh tears in her eyes. She smiled and tasted the saltiness of them as they streamed down her face. "Stay. Don't go. Stay in Clear Creek with me. And … and if you even think about trying to leave, Bowen Drake, I'll hunt you down and haul you back."

"I won't leave. I promise." And with that, Bowen Drake kissed Elsie Waller the way he'd wanted to kiss her all along.

And now the men in the audience let loose!

Christmas morning found Elsie Waller getting more than she'd bargained for. She discovered not only a beautiful silver comb and brush set under the tree, but a lovely necklace as well. But the best thing she found was the man she'd fallen in love with. A man she'd taken a leap of faith with – not by coming to believe he was innocent of bank robbery, but by trusting and allowing her own heart to love first, rather than wait until it seemed safe.

What would Bowen have done if she'd said nothing the night before? Would he have left? If he had, what would *she* have done? She really could see herself riding after him to tell him she loved him and drag him back. The thought of sitting and doing nothing would've pained her worse than any heartbreak could. A heart might heal in time, but regret stayed with a person the rest of their life, and that wasn't something she wanted.

"I don't have a ring for you yet," Bowen whispered into her hair as they sat on the settee in the parlor. "But come spring, I'll be able to afford one."

Elsie melted at the sound of his voice. She'd never tire of it – she could listen to him for the rest of her life. And planned to. "I can get along without one until then," she whispered back.

"Don't think this means I can wait to marry you until then. I'd marry you right here, right now if I could."

She smiled at that. "I don't have a ring or a dress, but at least I have you."

"One out of three ain't bad?" he chuckled.

"No, I suppose not. Besides, the Good Book doesn't say anything about Joseph or Mary having a ring." She turned to look at him. "What are we going to do once the hotel is finished?"

"You mean what'll I do for work? I might be able to wangle a job out at the Triple-C, but I'm …"

"You'll do no such thing, Bowen Drake!" Both Elsie and Bowen looked up to see Grandma standing in the doorway.

"But Grandma, it's all there is," Bowen told her.

"Oh no, it's not, and you know it!"

Bowen stiffened. He knew what was coming.

"You'll stay here and help Doc out. We're getting on in years, and we can't keep up with this town the way it's growing."

"Grandma," Elsie said. "What are you talking about?"

"I'm talking about this!" She held up an old newspaper.

"Oh no," Bowen groaned.

"Let me see," Elsie said, reaching out a hand. Grandma handed it to her, and she quickly spotted the article in question. "Good Lord! This is about the stage robbery from last year!"

" How did you come by this?" Bowen asked.

"Sheriff Hughes done gave it to me," Grandma explained. "He remembered reading about it after you told him, the night those scoundrels tried to get you to rob the bank."

"How did *he* get it? This isn't a local paper," Bowen said.

"A marshal had it on him and left it here. Sheriff Hughes was using it to line a desk drawer. We don't have us a paper here in Clear Creek, so the out-of-town ones come in mighty handy."

Bowen looked between Elsie and Grandma. "Well, it's nice to know some folks have found a better use for my heroic tales than I've ever had."

"But this paper also says who your father is, where you're from, where you went to school, and what the family business is," Elsie added.

Bowen gulped.

"You've been holding out on us, Bowen Drake," Grandma scolded.

Grandpa waltzed into the parlor, went to the candy

dish, and grabbed a peppermint. "You'll start working for me as soon as Mr. Van Cleet's done with ya. I may actually get to take up checkers again!"

"Wait a minute! Don't I have any say in this?" Bowen said, trying to keep the pleading in his voice to a minimum.

"NO!" they answered in unison.

Bowen looked at them all, and shrugged. "All right," he said in surrender. "Why should this be any different from the rest of my life?"

"Bowen," Elsie said softly. "Why wouldn't you want to be the town doctor? You're so good at it."

"Because I … I …" He looked at her. "Good Lord. I guess I don't have a reason not to anymore."

"Why would you have a reason not to in the first place?"

He looked at each of them in turn. "Because I thought I had to. Because I was angry and sad, and …" He let out a lengthy sigh. "… and it served me ill to stay that way."

"Ya can't run from your gifts, boy," Grandpa said. "They have a habit of following ya wherever you go."

Elsie reached up and pushed a lock of hair off Bowen's forehead. "Well, I for one am glad they followed you here."

Bowen smiled, took her in his arms and kissed her. "So am I, my future wife. So am I."

The End

Dear Reader ~

I hope you enjoyed **Christmas in Clear Creek.** That wraps up the Prairie Brides Series, but the story's still not over – be sure to check out the further adventures of the folks in Clear Creek with the Prairie Grooms Series, available now!

(And if you still need something for your Christmas sweet tooth, take a look at **The Christmas Mail-Order Bride** and get to know Clayton and Spencer Riley, the brothers Elsie talks about in **Christmas in Clear Creek** from her hometown in Nowhere, Washington. It's also the first book of its own series, The Holiday Mail-Order Brides!)

Kit Morgan

About the Author

KIT MORGAN, AKA GERALYN BEAUCHAMP, lives in a log cabin in the woods in the wonderful state of Oregon. She grew up riding horses, playing cowboys and Indians and has always had a love of Westerns! She and her father watched many Western movies and television shows together, and enjoyed the quirky characters of *Green Acres* as well. One of her father's favorite comedic television shows. Thus, Kit's books have been described as "*Green Acres* meets *Gunsmoke*," and have brought joy and entertainment to thousands of readers. Many of her books are now in audio format and performed by a talented voice actor who brings Kit's characters to life, and can be found on Amazon, Audible.com and iTunes.

You can keep up-to-date on future books, fun contests and more by signing up for Kit's newsletter at www.authorkitmorgan.com

CPSIA information can be obtained
at www.ICGtesting.com
Printed in the USA
LVHW110456160622
721422LV00004B/137

9 781539 148128